D0941586

# FUNNY
# YOU
# SHOULD
# ASK

# FUNNY YOU SHOULD ASK

## THE DELACORTE BOOK OF ORIGINAL HUMOROUS SHORT STORIES

Edited by David Gale

Delacorte
Press

Published by
Delacorte Press
Bantam Doubleday Dell Publishing Group, Inc.
666 Fifth Avenue
New York, New York 10103

Library of Congress Cataloging in Publication Data
Funny you should ask : the Delacorte book of original humorous short stories
/ edited by David Gale.
p.  cm.
Summary: A collection of sixteen humorous stories, grouped under the
headings "All in the Family," "That's What Friends Are For," and
"Classrooms and Corridors."
ISBN 0-385-30535-4
1. Children's stories, American. 2. Humorous stories, American. [1. Humorous
stories. 2. Short stories.] I. Gale, David, 1955–. II. Title: Delacorte book of
original humorous short stories.
PZ5.F968 1992
[Fic]—dc20                                                                              91-15848
                                                                                              CIP
                                                                                               AC

Manufactured in the United States of America
April 1992

10  9  8  7  6  5  4  3  2  1
BVG

For Max and Zoe

# CONTENTS

# CONTENTS

# INTRODUCTION

Have you heard the one about the duck who bought some Chap Stick? The clerk asked, "Will this be cash or charge?" and the duck answered, "Just put it on my bill."

Everyone likes a joke, but humor comes in many forms. Each of the stories in this collection is funny, but in very different ways. From the droll to the ludicrous, from the sublime to the ridiculous, the stories here are in turn amusing, witty, absurd, clever, comic, or farcical. A full range of humorous writing can be found in these sixteen stories.

In addition to being humorous, each of these stories has been written by a prominent American author of books for children. Among the writers represented in this collection are Newbery Honor Book award winners, authors whose books have been named Notable Books for Children or Best Books for Young Adults by the American Library Association, writers whose books have been highlighted as the best of the year by ALA's *Booklist* or by *School Library Journal,* authors whose books have been honored by child and parent selectors, and writers whose books have received numerous other honors. These are among the finest writers working today.

In this collection, you will find some of your favorite authors. In fact, some of the writers have chosen to write about a character who has already appeared in books that they have written. Their short stories will allow you to find out more about those characters. This collection will also introduce you to some authors who will be new to you. At the end of each story, you will find a biographical or autobiographical statement, which will cite other books by the author that you might want to read next.

The authors whose work appears here were invited, along with many other writers, to submit short stories to this anthology. I chose authors whose writing I admire. Not all of them are known for their humorous books—although many of them are—but all were willing to rise to the challenge. The contributors were given very few rules. First, the stories had to be original to this collection, never before published. Second, they had to be honest-to-goodness short stories, with a beginning, a middle, and an end. Excerpts from longer works were not considered. Third, and most important, the stories had to be funny.

I want to publicly thank all of the authors who graciously agreed to submit a story to this collection. Unfortunately, not all of the stories that were submitted could be accepted, but I am grateful for the authors' willingness to take part in this project and for having had the chance to consider their stories. All royalties generated by the sale of this book are being donated to the Association for Library Service to Children (ALSC), a division of the American Library Association, to be applied toward the Distinguished Service to ALSC Award.

The stories in this book include one about a young

## INTRODUCTION

boy who can think of nothing but making money, a ghost story in which a practical joke backfires, a fable about a boy who tries everything to get rid of a bothersome itch, and a holiday tale about the darker side of family gatherings. They are loosely grouped by the relationships among the main characters and the settings —the widening circles of family, friends, and school.

I wanted this collection to include only funny stories because humor is frequently requested by readers, but truly funny writing is often hard to find.

So, do you want to read a short story and have a good laugh? Funny you should ask . . .

# ALL IN THE FAMILY

Relatives! You can't live with them,
and you can't live without them.

• • • • • • • • • •

# THANKSGIVING IN POLYNESIA

## Susan Haven

**I** place my palms on the
window ledge of the huge double window in my mom
and dad's bedroom, and hoist myself up until I am
kneeling on the sill, my nose to the window.

Beyond, and three feet below, is my backyard.

It's not fair. I cleaned my room, I swear I did.

I made my bed, picked up the stuff on the floor, and
put all my books in the bookshelf.

But did my mom thank me? Of course not.

Just because I shoved the Monopoly pieces under
the bed, along with a couple of nightgowns and maybe
two or three CDs that lost their cases, she got mad.

Picky, picky, picky.

First she told me, "I want your room cleaned in an

hour," and then when I tried a time-saving plan, like storing stuff under the bed, she didn't appreciate it.

A little bad luck made things even worse.

When she came in to check on me, she stepped barefoot on a little metal Monopoly token.

Wow. Does she scream loud.

I apologized and everything.

But did she forgive me? Of course not.

I'm going to jump out this window, then sneak around the alley and crawl on my stomach past the big kitchen window. My mom's in the kitchen right now, with my aunt Rhea, getting the Thanksgiving dinner ready, and I don't want them to see me make my escape.

My aunt is why my mom's in such a bad mood, I know it.

She and my uncle Ted, and their one perfect kid, Andrea (my age, ten and a half) arrived from Chicago this morning.

We're all supposed to break turkey together in about half an hour.

I plan to be in Polynesia. Or at least New Jersey, by then.

Our family is not too fond of their family, but they come every Thanksgiving anyway.

My mom especially dislikes my aunt Rhea. She's rich and snobby and makes my mom and dad and my older brother, Jason, and me feel terrible.

She speaks with an English accent, even though I know she was born right here, where we live, in Massapequa, Long Island, New York.

Whenever Jason or I turn on the TV, Aunt Rhea always asks, oh so sweetly, "My, my, don't you two watch a dreadfully large quantity of television?"

That's the Rhea technique: questions that kill.

Like this morning, she asked Jason, when he was grabbing a cookie from the cookie jar: "Wouldn't you prefer a carrot?"

Who'd prefer a carrot to one of my mom's chocolate-chip cookies, anyway?

Or later, as my mom was setting the big table, Rhea came over with the napkins and said: "My, my, Sara, but don't you make Missy or Jason do anything around here?"

Jason calls her Aunt Dia-Rhea.

Unfortunately, my mom brought her into my room to show her how I'd cleaned up before they all arrived, and that's when my mom stepped on the Monopoly top hat. And called me a slob. In front of Aunt Rhea. And told me not to come out until my room is spotless.

My first plan was not to come out of my room until I'm eighteen.

But that didn't seem possible. So I snuck in here, to my parents' bedroom, in the back of the house, and I'm going to climb out this window.

I'd have snuck out of mine, but I left some candies on my window ledge and they melted onto the metal window and now it won't open so easily.

More bad luck.

Besides, I don't want to play with my cousin Andrea anymore.

She is what my grandmother calls "a lovely child."

Andrea offered to set the table.

She always picks up her dishes after a meal and puts them in the sink.

She does the laundry every Saturday.

She compliments everybody on everything.

She doesn't even have to be reminded to do that stuff.

Personally, I think that's sick.

And when we started to play a game of jacks, she slaughtered me. And apologized every move she made.

I press my nose to the window. In the distance, I can see Annie MacElvane's house.

My best friend.

She is probably sitting down to Thanksgiving dinner right now with her warm, friendly family.

I could run away there.

It's not Polynesia, but as my dad would say, I'd make good time. I'd be there in a sec.

The problem is—I can't run anywhere until I get the summer screen out of this window.

I'd rather run away to Polynesia, because it's a great place for kids.

We just studied it in Mrs. Schwartz's Cultures of the World unit.

There's no such word in Polynesia as *my* or *our*. Those are called possessive pronouns. The reason they don't have possessive pronouns is that nobody owns anything, including their own children. Children belong to God and the land and the universe. They have total freedom.

# THANKSGIVING IN POLYNESIA

According to my map, Polynesia is about six inches from America. Which can't be that far.

I wonder what the kids in Polynesia are like.

I wonder if when they're in school, they have a unit called "The Peoples of Massapequa."

As a token of my friendliness, I'm bringing my jacks along. Mrs. Schwartz says that when you visit other peoples, you should bring a symbol of your own peoples. Jacks should do it. Plus, they'll give me something to do until I make a friend.

Well, the sooner I leave, the sooner I'll be playing tensies in paradise.

Maybe I'll just shove this screen right out the window.

Scrunching down, I kick at it.

Uh oh. A hole. The screen's still attached, but now there's this big hole in it that's the shape of my foot.

If I weren't running away already, I'd seriously consider it now, because when they discover this little disaster I'll be grounded until college.

I'll have to make the hole just a little bigger. Girl size.

Perfect. I'm set.

When my mom and dad realize I'm gone, their hearts will break.

In fact, I think I should write a note to make them feel a little worse. Something like:

> Dear Mom and Dad: This home is not working out. If you miss me, call Polynesia 2-4000.

Or:

> Personally, I've had enough. I'm going to
> Polynesia. Don't worry about the sharks
> there. I'll be fine.

If a shark eats me, that'll really kill them.

My body is easing into the scratchy screen when suddenly I hear a *thud.*

A *thump.*

A *clump.*

And then the rattle and vibration of furniture in the hall.

Heavy footsteps are coming toward the bedroom.

My body stiffens. My heart pounds.

Who could that be? I have to get out of here. Fast.

Ow. The torn screen is so scratchy.

*Thud. Rattle. Tickle.*

*Bounce. Bounce.*

It's my brother, Jason. Bouncing a basketball in the hall.

When my mom yells at him about indoor basketball bouncing, she has a point. The whole house vibrates.

Is that the doorknob turning? This doorknob?

I try to ease my body further through the screen.

I can't get out.

There's only one thing I can do.

Backing my butt out of the screen, I jump down from the ledge and look around my mom's room for a place to hide.

The closet.

I'll never make it in time.

Diving onto the floor, I roll under the huge queen-size bed just as the door opens.

In a second, I'm peeking out from under the bedspread, inches from Jason's big clodhopper feet, which are now standing in front of my mom's bureau.

I bet he's looking in the mirror, as usual.

Wait. Those clodhoppers of his are moving. Is he leaving?

No. He's moving toward the window.

I peek out a little further just in time to see him climb onto the ledge, open the window, and kick the screen right out into the backyard.

"What does she want," he's muttering. "I went to the store. I meant to buy regular milk. So I didn't see the label that said buttermilk. Personally, I've had enough!"

His leg is out the window.

My gosh.

He's running away too!

Gee. I'm going to miss him.

What am I talking about—I'm going to miss him? I'm running away too!

*Thud. Thud.*

It's footsteps again.

What is this? A convention?

You can't even have a little privacy in your own parents' bedroom when you want it.

Jason's heard something too. His head is turned, perked at attention.

The doorknob. It's turning again.

Jason's eyes widen in panic and then he jumps backward off the window ledge.

The next thing I know, I have company under the bed.

"Happy Thanksgiving . . ." I whisper.

*"Ahhh!"* he almost screams in fright, but I cover his mouth as I swallow a giggle, because we can both hear the soft *clip clap* of my mom's loose slippers.

She's *clip clapping* around the room. The bureau drawer squeaks open, there's the soft *whoosh* of something being removed, the drawer squeaks shut again, and then the springs of the mattress hit my nose as she plops down on the bed.

She's sighing. Which lowers the springs even more.

Then she mutters, "Personally, I've had enough . . ." and leans backward. "On the other hand, you're a grown woman, Sara. Now, go out there and handle it."

The springs lower, hitting me in the nose, and then lift.

She's gotten up.

In a second, we hear the door open and softly shut.

She's gone.

Wait a second. It's opening again.

"Sara? Are you in here?"

It's my dad, coming in.

But where's my mom, if my dad didn't see her going out?

I know I heard the door shutting.

Oh no. It couldn't be.

But it is.

The door that shut wasn't the bedroom door.

It was the closet door.

My mom, my thirty-five-year-old mom, is hiding in the closet at this very moment.

"Sara? Jason? Missy?" my dad whispers again in a voice that sounds a little lonely.

Gee. Poor Daddy.

He's been stuck out there all alone with Aunt Rhea and Uncle Ted.

Uncle Ted probably just finished showing off his newest gold charge cards to my dad.

I peek out from underneath the bottom of the bedspread.

Everything that's going on is reflected in the full-length mirror on the closet door. I can see a dress caught in the doorjamb of my mom's closet.

She's in there all right.

"Where is everybody?" my dad says.

Silence.

My dad takes one last look around the room, and then moves to the bedroom door again.

But just as he's backing out, the closet door opens and my mom pops out.

"Hi . . ." she says.

"Sara! What are you doing in the closet?"

"I was . . . I was looking for a better tablecloth." She swallows and then continues. "Actually, I was also looking for a whole new house. And a whole new me. But . . . it's not in there. . . ." Her face starts to pucker, like she's going to cry.

My dad puts his arm around her.

"Is Rhea getting to you, honey?"

My mom shakes her head. "Nooo. What makes you think that?"

My dad grins.

"And I took it out on the kids. . . ."

"They'll live. . . ." my dad says.

Sure we'll live, I think. But where?

"What's the matter with me?" my mom sobs. "I'm a grown woman. Why does that phony get to me? Why can't I handle it? I have no character. No courage. No strength. You want me to make it all nice. And I try, but she's getting to me. Even your brother Ted is getting to me. All his mutual funds are going up. Did you know that?"

My dad nods. "Sure did."

"Plus, I've been yelling at the kids. For nothing. Well, not nothing. . . ."

Nothing, Mom. Nothing.

"And they're fed up with me. And I don't blame them." She starts to cry again. "The turkey is probably dry, I have an ugly tablecloth, and I'm a terrible mother." She's bawling.

I have to admit that the sound of my mom's sobs is getting to me. I can't help it.

"You're not *such* a terrible mother . . ." I mumble.

The sobbing stops.

"Who's that? Where's that? What's that?" my mom asks.

"Stevie Baldwin's mom is worse," Jason talks right into the mattress. "She's not as mean as you are today, but she treats him like a baby. Last week, four guys were playing pool in his room, and she walks in, and with this high, squeaky voice, says 'Would any of you boys like a Twinkie . . . ?' You'd never do that!"

Just as Jason's finishing his speech the bedspread,

like a curtain, rises, and my mom's wide eyes stare at us.

"Happy Thanksgiving," I say to her. Then, I can't help adding, "But for next Thanksgiving, you ought to dust under here, Mom. . . ."

She blushes. Then her thumb jerks backward, like a hitchhiker.

"Out. Both of you. Out."

Jason rolls one way. I roll the other.

In a second we're all standing around my mom and dad's bed.

My mom's fingertips are against her cheeks. I think she's in shock. My dad's eyes have already taken in the open window.

Just as I say, "Jason was running away," Jason says "Missy was running away."

And then we both say, "We can't take it anymore either."

My dad and mom give each other looks. I feel lectures and meaningless sayings coming on.

"Aunt Rhea means well . . ." my mom begins.

But now that we know how she really feels about Aunt Rhea, all we have to do is give her a "yeah, sure" look, and she stops.

"On the other hand, kids . . ." Now my dad is going into speech mode. "You can't run away from a problem. . . ."

But then he looks at my mom, who is standing inches from her former hideaway closet.

And he stops. And sighs. "What are we going to do?" he says. "They are unbearable. I've tried to talk to them, hint, be diplomatic, but it's like talking to Martians . . ."

Everyone's looking dumb, so I jump right in there. "Could we . . . *all* run away?" I ask softly.

All our eyes shift to the open window. Then we look at each other.

I can see the open sea. Polynesia. Palm trees.

Then my dad sighs. "My mother, your grandmother, would have a heart attack in heaven. . . . I can't . . ."

My mom agrees. "Look, it's a Thanksgiving from hell . . . but otherwise it's not *so* terrible. What we have to do is what we do every year. Get through it, and give thanks on Sunday—when it's over."

Everybody nods at practically the same time. Which makes us all giggle.

"Are we ready?" my dad asks. "We have to get out there or they're going to start to get suspicious. Plus, the turkey is done. . . ."

My mother turns white. "Oh my God . . . my turkey . . . my turkey." She lunges for the door.

Then she stops, pauses, looks back at us, puts a big smile on her face, stands up straight, and with dignity, walks out her bedroom door.

My father follows.

My brother goes next.

Before I leave, I take one last peek at the window.

I guess that's what people mean by a window of opportunity.

Polynesia would have been swell.

But it's not to be.

Of course, Christmas is coming up and there are rumors that my mother's second cousins are coming up from Florida.

I can feel the wind wafting through my hair already.

But in the meanwhile, I close the door behind me, take a deep breath, and gather up the courage that the Peoples of Massapequa are known for.

# About Susan Haven

•••••••

I have been a comedy writer for twenty years, writing humorous articles for a variety of publications (*The New York Times, Ms.* Magazine, *Glamour, Cosmopolitan, Redbook,* etc.) and comedy for television and the movies (*All in the Family, Facts of Life,* Lily Tomlin).

My first young adult book, *Maybe I'll Move to the Lost and Found,* is about Gilly Miles, a girl who wants to be like either of her two best friends—Victory, an outrageous, courageous, unconventional, zany filmmaker who isn't afraid to offend anybody—or Franny, the sweetest, prettiest, most popular girl at Gilly's junior high. In the middle of her confusion, the father she loved and who walked out on her family moves right back in with his girlfriend, Airhead.

My second book, *Is It Me or Is It Them,* is about how another young teenager, Molly Snyder, handles a totally impossible teacher; a loving, but ill mother; and a brother who has been torturing her ever since he gave her her first wrist burn in her bassinet.

Being funny gets my characters through whatever crisis they need to get through, and it's helped me as well. I'm grateful that I live with a son and a husband who can easily make me laugh, no matter what. I am also a social worker, working as a therapist with families. Besides my family, nothing gives me more pleasure than being around or working with kids.

It's no fun having to baby-sit
your brother all summer long.
Still, you shouldn't *lose* him.

• • • • • • • • • •

# THE TAIL

## Joyce Hansen

**I**t began as the worst summer of my life. The evening before the first day of summer vacation, my mother broke the bad news to me. I was in the kitchen washing dishes and dreaming about the wonderful things my friends and I would be doing for two whole months—practicing for the annual double-dutch contest, which we would definitely win; going to the roller skating rink, the swimming pool, the beach; and sleeping as late in the morning as I wanted to.

"Tasha," my ma broke into my happy thoughts, "your father and I decided that you're old enough now to take on certain responsibilities."

My heart came to a sudden halt. "Responsibilities?"

"Yes. You do know what that word means, don't you?"

I nodded, watching her dice an onion into small, perfect pieces.

"You're thirteen going on fourteen and your father and I decided that you're old enough to watch Junior this summer, because I'm going to start working again."

"Oh, no!" I broke the dish with a crash. "Not that, Mama." Junior is my seven-year-old brother and has been following me like a tail ever since he learned how to walk. And to make matters worse, there are no kids Junior's age on our block. Everyone is either older or younger than he is.

I'd rather be in school than minding Junior all day. I could've cried.

"Natasha! There won't be a dish left in this house. You're not going to spend all summer ripping and roaring. You'll baby-sit Junior."

"But, Ma," I said, "it'll be miserable. That's not fair. All summer with Junior. I won't be able to play with my friends."

She wiped her hands on her apron. "Life ain't always fair."

I knew she'd say that.

"You'll still be able to play with your friends," she continued, "but Junior comes first. He is your responsibility. We're a family and we all have to help out."

Mama went to work that next morning. Junior and I both stood by the door as she gave her last-minute instructions. Junior held her hand and stared up at her with an innocent look in his bright brown eyes, which everyone thought were so cute. Dimples decorated his round cheeks as he smiled and nodded at me every time Ma gave me an order. I knew he was just waiting for her to leave so he could torment me.

"Tasha, I'm depending on you. Don't leave the block."

"Yes, Ma."

"No company."

"Not even Naomi? She's my best friend."

"No company when your father and I are not home."

"Yes, Ma."

"Don't let Junior hike in the park."

"Yes, Ma."

"Make yourself and Junior a sandwich for lunch."

"Yes, Ma."

"I'll be calling you at twelve, so you'd better be in here fixing lunch. I don't want you all eating junk food all day long."

"Yes, Ma."

"Don't ignore Junior."

"Yes, Ma."

"Clean the breakfast dishes."

"Yes, Ma."

"Don't open the door to strangers."

"Yes, Ma."

Then she turned to Junior. "Now you, young man. You are to listen to your sister."

"Yes, Mommy," he sang out.

"Don't give her a hard time. Show me what a big boy you can be."

"Mommy, I'll do whatever Tasha say."

She kissed us both good-bye and left. I wanted to cry. A whole summer with Junior.

Junior turned to me and raised his right hand. "This is a vow of obedience." He looked up at the ceiling. "I promise to do whatever Tasha says."

"What do you know about vows?" I asked.

"I saw it on television. A man—"

"Shut up, Junior. I don't feel like hearing about some television show. It's too early in the morning."

I went into the kitchen to start cleaning, when the downstairs bell rang. "Answer the intercom, Junior. If it's Naomi, tell her to wait for me on the stoop," I called out. I knew that it was Naomi, ready to start our big, fun summer. After a few minutes the bell rang again.

"Junior!" I yelled. "Answer the intercom."

The bell rang again and I ran into the living room. Junior was sitting on the couch, looking at cartoons. "What's wrong with you? Why won't you answer the bell?"

He looked at me as if I were crazy. "You told me to shut up. I told you I'd do everything you say."

I pulled my hair. "See, you're bugging me already. Do something to help around here."

I pressed the intercom on the wall. "That you, Naomi?"

"Yeah."

"I'll be down in a minute. Wait for me out front."

"Okay."

I quickly washed the dishes. I couldn't believe how messed up my plans were. Suddenly there was a loud blast from the living room. I was so startled that I dropped a plate and it smashed to smithereens. Ma will kill me, I thought as I ran to the living room. It sounded like whole pieces of furniture were being sucked into the vacuum cleaner.

"Junior," I screamed over the racket, "you have it on too high."

He couldn't even hear me. I turned it off myself.

"What's wrong?"

"Ma vacuumed the living room last night. It doesn't need cleaning."

"You told me to do something to help," he whined.

I finished the dishes in a hurry so that I could leave the apartment before Junior bugged out again.

I was so anxious to get outside that we ran down the four flights of stairs instead of waiting for the elevator. Junior clutched some comic books and his checkers game. He put his Mets baseball cap on backward as usual. Naomi sat on the stoop and Junior plopped right next to her like they were the best of friends.

"Hi, cutey." She smiled at him, turning his cap to the front of his head the way it was supposed to be. "What are we going to do today, Naomi?" he asked.

"Junior, you're not going to be in our faces all day," I snapped at him.

"Mama said you have to watch me. So I have to be in your face."

"You're baby-sitting, Tasha?" Naomi asked.

"Yeah." I told her the whole story.

"Aw, that's not so bad. At least you don't have to stay in the house. Junior will be good. Right, cutey?"

He grinned as she pinched his cheeks.

"See, you think he's cute because you don't have no pesty little brother or sister to watch," I grumbled.

"You ready for double-dutch practice?" she asked. "Yvonne and Keisha are going to meet us in the playground."

"Mama said we have to stay on the block," Junior answered before I could even open my mouth.

"No one's talking to you, Junior." I pulled Naomi up off the stoop. "I promised my mother we'd stay on the block, but the playground is just across the street. I can see the block from there."

"It's still not the block," Junior mumbled as we raced across the street.

We always went over to the playground to jump rope. The playground was just by the entrance to the park. There was a lot of space for us to do our fancy steps. The park was like a big green mountain in the middle of Broadway.

I'd figure out a way to keep Junior from telling that we really didn't stay on the block. "Hey, Tasha, can I go inside the park and look for caves?" People said that if you went deep inside the park, there were caves that had been used centuries ago when Native Americans still lived in northern Manhattan.

"No, Ma said no hiking in the park."

"She said no leaving the block, too, and you left the block."

"Look how close we are to the block. I mean, we can even see it. You could get lost inside the park."

"I'm going to tell Ma you didn't stay on the block."

"Okay, me and Naomi will hike with you up to the Cloisters later." That's a museum that sits at the top of the park, overlooking the Hudson River. "Now read your comic books."

"Will you play checkers with me too?"

"You know I hate checkers. Leave me alone." I spotted Keisha and Yvonne walking into the playground. All of us wore shorts and sneakers.

Junior tagged behind me and Naomi as we went to meet them. "Remember you're supposed to be watching me," he said.

"How could I forget."

The playground was crowded. Swings were all taken and the older boys played stickball. Some little kids played in the sandboxes.

Keisha and Yvonne turned and Naomi and I jumped together, practicing a new routine. We were so good that some of the boys in the stickball game watched us. A few elderly people stopped to look at us too. We had an audience, so I really showed off—spinning and doing a lot of fancy footwork.

Suddenly Junior jumped in the ropes with us and people laughed and clapped.

"Junior!" I screamed. "Get out of here!"

"Remember, your job is to watch me." He grinned. My foot slipped and all three of us got tangled in the ropes and fell.

"Your feet are too big!" Junior yelled.

Everybody roared. I was too embarrassed. I tried to grab him, but he got away from me. "Get lost," I hollered after him as he ran toward the swings.

I tried to forget how stupid I must've looked and went back to the ropes. I don't know how long we'd been jumping when suddenly a little kid ran by us yelling, "There's a wild dog loose up there!" He pointed to the steps that led deep inside the park.

People had been saying for years that a pack of abandoned dogs who'd turned wild lived in the park, but no one ever really saw them.

We forgot about the kid and kept jumping. Then one of the boys our age who'd been playing stickball came over to us. "We're getting out of here," he said. "A big yellow dog with red eyes just bit a kid."

I took the rope from Yvonne. It was time for me and Naomi to turn. "That's ridiculous. Who ever heard of a yellow dog with red eyes?"

Naomi stopped turning. "Dogs look all kind of ways. Especially wild dogs. I'm leaving."

"Me too," Yvonne said.

Keisha was already gone. No one was in the swings or the sandboxes. I didn't even see the old men who usually sat on the benches. "Guess we'd better get out of here too," I said. Then I realized that I didn't see Junior anywhere.

"Junior!" I shouted.

"Maybe he went home," Naomi said.

We dashed across the street. Our block was empty. Yvonne ran ahead of us and didn't stop until she reached her stoop. When I got to my stoop I expected to see Junior there, but no Junior.

"Maybe he went upstairs," Naomi said.

"I have the key. He can't get in the house."

"Maybe he went to the candy store?"

"He doesn't have any money, I don't think. But let's look."

We ran around the corner to the candy store, but no Junior.

As we walked back to the block, I remembered something.

"Oh, no, Naomi, I told him to get lost. And that's just what he did."

"He's probably hiding from us somewhere. You know how he likes to tease." She looked around as we walked up our block. "He might be hiding and watching us right now looking for him." She peeped behind parked cars, in doorways, and even opened the lid of a trash can.

"Junior," I called. "Junior!"

No answer. Only the sounds of birds and cars, sirens and a distant radio. I looked at the empty stoop where Junior should have been sitting. A part of me was gone and I had to find it. And another part of me would be gone if my mother found out I'd lost Junior.

I ran back toward the playground and Naomi followed me. "He's got to be somewhere right around here," she panted.

I ran past the playground and into the park. "Tasha, you're not going in there, are you? The dog."

I didn't answer her and began climbing the stone steps that wound around and through the park. Naomi's eyes stretched all over her face and she grabbed my arm. "It's dangerous up here!"

I turned around. "If you're scared, don't come. Junior's my only baby brother. Dear God," I said out loud, "please let me find him. I will play any kind of game he wants. I'll never yell at him again. I promise never to be mean to him again in my life!"

Naomi breathed heavily behind me. "I don't think Junior would go this far by himself."

I stopped and caught my breath. The trees were thick and the city street sounds were far away now.

"I know Junior. He's somewhere up here making believe he's the king of this mountain. Hey, Junior," I called, "I was just kidding. Don't get lost." We heard a rustling in the bushes and grabbed each other. "Probably just a bird," I said, trying to sound brave.

As we climbed some more, I tried not to imagine a huge yellow dog with red eyes gnawing at my heels.

The steps turned a corner and ended. Naomi screamed and pointed up ahead. "What's that?"

I saw a big brown and gray monstrous thing with tentacles reaching toward the sky, jutting out of the curve in the path. I screamed and almost ran.

"What is that, Naomi?"

"I don't know."

"This is a park in the middle of Manhattan. It can't be a bear or anything." I screamed to the top of my lungs, "Junior!" Some birds flew out of a tree, but the thing never moved.

All Naomi could say was, "Dogs, Tasha."

I found a stick. "I'm going up. You wait here. If you hear growling and screaming, run and get some help." I couldn't believe how brave I was. Anyway, that thing, whatever it was, couldn't hurt me any more than my mother would if I didn't find Junior.

"You sure, Tasha?"

"No sense in both of us being mauled," I said.

I tipped lightly up the steps, holding the stick like a club. When I was a few feet away from the thing, I crumpled to the ground and laughed so hard that Naomi ran to me. "Naomi, look at what scared us." She laughed too. "A dead tree trunk." We both laughed until we cried. Then I saw one of Junior's comic books near a bush. I picked it up and started to cry. "See, he was here. And that animal probably tore him to pieces." Naomi patted my shaking shoulders.

Suddenly, there was an unbelievable growl. My legs turned to air as I flew down the steps. Naomi was ahead of me. Her two braids stuck out like propellers. My feet didn't even touch the ground. We screamed all the way down the steps. I tripped on the last step and was sprawled out on the ground. Two women passing by bent over me. "Child, are you hurt?" one of them asked.

Then I heard a familiar laugh above me and looked up into Junior's dimpled face. He laughed so hard, he held his stomach with one hand. His checkers game was in the other. A little tan, mangy dog stood next to him, wagging its tail.

I got up slowly. "Junior, I'm going to choke you."

He doubled over with squeals and chuckles. I wiped my filthy shorts with one hand and stretched out the other to snatch Junior's neck. The stupid little dog had the nerve to growl.

"Me and Thunder hid in the bushes. We followed you." He continued laughing. Then he turned to the dog. "Thunder, didn't Tasha look funny holding that stick like she was going to beat up the tree trunk?"

I put my hands around Junior's neck. "This is the end of the tail," I said.

Junior grinned. "You promised. 'I'll play any game he wants. I'll never yell at him again. I promise never to be mean to him again in my life.' "

Naomi giggled. "That's what you said, Tasha." The mutt barked at me. Guess he called himself Junior's protector. I took my hands off Junior's neck.

Then Naomi had a laughing spasm. She pointed at the dog. "Is that what everyone was running from?"

"This is my trusted guard. People say he's wild. He just wants a friend."

"Thunder looks like he's already got a lot of friends living inside his fur," I said. We walked back to the block with the dog trotting right by Junior's side.

I checked my watch when we got to my building. "It's ten to twelve. I have to make lunch for Junior," I told Naomi. "But I'll be back out later."

The dog whined after Junior as we entered the building. "I'll be back soon, Thunder," he said, "after I beat my sister in five games of checkers."

Now he was going to blackmail me.

I heard Naomi giggling as Junior and I walked into the building. The phone rang just as we entered the apartment. I knew it was Ma.

"Everything okay, Tasha? Nothing happened?"

"No, Ma, everything is fine. Nothing happened at all."

Well, the summer didn't turn out to be so terrible after all. My parents got Thunder cleaned up and let Junior keep him for a pet. Me and my friends practiced for the double-dutch contest right in front of my building, so I didn't have to leave the block. After lunch when it was too hot to jump rope, I'd play a game of checkers with Junior or read him a story. He wasn't as pesty as he used to be, because now he had Thunder. We won the double-dutch contest. And Junior never told my parents that I'd lost him. I found out that you never miss a tail until you almost lose it.

# About Joyce Hansen

• • • • • • •

I have been writing novels and stories for young people for the past thirteen years. My first novel was *The Gift Giver*, followed by *Yellow Bird and Me*, *Home Boy*, *Which Way Freedom?*, and *Out from This Place*. *Which Way Freedom?* won a Coretta Scott King Honor Book Award in 1987. I am currently working on a nonfiction book about black soldiers in the Civil War and have recently completed a historical novel.

The story "The Tail" was based in some ways on my own experiences growing up in the Bronx with two younger brothers. One of my brothers once befriended a stray dog that everyone else on the block was running away from. I often base my stories and characterizations on incidents and people from my own life.

There are over eight million stories
in New York City, and Mr. Rabinowitz
the taxicab driver hears them all.

• • • • • • • • • • •

# THE TAXICAB FAMILY

## Barbara Ann Porte

**A**bigail and Sam Rabino-
witz live with their parents, Rita and Al, and a black
dachshund named Benton, on the tenth floor of a high-
rise apartment in lower Manhattan. Their mother
works at home, translating Russian-language books
into English. Their father used to do the same, but now
he drives a taxicab. "The pay is more dependable. Plus
you get to meet such interesting people," he says. Frequently, when he comes home from work he tells his
family about his fares; only the highlights. His wife is
glad for any adult conversation. "Also, it gives the children something to talk about in school," she explains
to Benton when only the two of them are in the apartment.

Last Wednesday at dinner, finishing a second helping of apple pie, Al Rabinowitz told his family this. "Today, a very fat woman and a very skinny woman got into my cab, each one carrying a duffel bag. They were on their way home from exercise class. 'You wouldn't believe it to look at us, but we used to be the other way around,' the fat woman said. 'I beg your pardon,' I said. The skinny woman nodded, and took some snapshots out of her pocketbook to show me. I looked them over at the first red light. I had to look twice. It certainly was true. In the photographs, the very fat woman in my cab was very skinny, and the very skinny one was very fat. 'What happened?' I asked. 'We joined a self-help group. It helped me eat more,' the very fat woman said. 'It helped me eat less,' the skinny woman added. 'After some time had passed, we changed places.' "

"How awful that must have been for the skinny one," Rita Rabinowitz said, pushing aside her slice of pie. She meant, of course, the skinny one in the photograph, and not in the cab.

"I thought that, too, at first," said her husband. "But apparently not. 'The best part is, we're the same height exactly,' both women told me. They seemed very pleased."

"Well, of course they're the same height," said Abigail. "Dieting doesn't change that."

"Right," said her father. "What they meant was, they were exactly the same height as each other. They didn't have to go out and buy all new clothing. 'We only had to trade wardrobes,' they explained happily."

"I see," said Abigail's mother. "They didn't happen

to mention whether they still belonged to the same self-help group, did they?"

"As a matter of fact, they did," her husband told her. "They were on their way home from a meeting when I picked them up."

Sam interrupted. "I thought you said they were coming from exercise class."

"Right," said his father. "Same group, new direction. 'It isn't what you weigh, but how you feel about it. Exercise puts a person in touch with her body,' the skinny woman said. The fat woman agreed. 'See, all those years when I was thin, there was a fat woman inside me screaming to get out. I couldn't hear her for dieting. Self-help exercise class enhances our image.' "

"Well, sure it does," said Sam, who exercises himself, hoping to get taller. The next day, in art class, he drew this picture: two women, one fat and one thin, dressed in leotards and tights, doing sit-ups in front of a mirror. Only, their reflections were reversed.

"Nice work, Sam, but your mirror needs turning," his art teacher said. Sam reexamined his picture. He left the mirror as it was, but added a caption, "Before and After."

"It's an interesting picture, but which is which?" Abigail asked when she saw it. Abigail's older than Sam. He was surprised at the need to explain.

"It's the fat woman before and the thin woman after," he told her. "Or you could look at it the other way around." He taped his drawing to the refrigerator door when he got home.

"Do you think it's a warning?" Ms. Rabinowitz asked Mr. Rabinowitz that night. He didn't claim to know, but the following evening he chose fruit over ice cream for dessert, and told a different sort of story.

"It's a dog story," he said as he started. Benton jumped onto his lap. "It's not about you, and you aren't a lap dog," Mr. Rabinowitz told him, but allowed him to stay.

"Benton likes dog stories," said Sam.

"Shhh," said Abigail, who liked dog stories herself. "Let Daddy tell it." Their father did.

"Today, a woman got into my cab with a very large dog. 'I'm sorry, animals are not allowed,' I told her. I started to explain that I like dogs myself, but some passengers don't care to get animal hairs on their clothing. The woman wasn't listening. She was pointing to the sign in my window: 'No pets, blind guide dogs only.'

" 'Yes, but you don't look blind,' I said.

" 'Not me. Sophie is blind. Sophie's my dog,' she told me. 'She's a Saint Bernard, the kind trained to guide rescue teams to travelers trapped in snow. She's retired now. She's very old. She's an old, blind guide dog; a bit hard of hearing too.' "

"What did you do?" asked Abigail.

"I drove them uptown. What else could I do? Afterward, I took the cab for a cleaning. It wasn't so bad. While I waited, I heard a story."

"What sort of a story?" asked Sam.

"A rainy day sort of a story," his father answered.

It rained in the morning. Their father fried eggs with onions for breakfast and told them this tale.

"The minute I put my cab in line to get cleaned, and got out, I saw Joe Sabatini. You remember him. He's the chorus-line dancer we went to see. He drives a cab when he's between shows. He looked a teensy bit droopy. 'It's nothing,' he told me. 'Last night I was tied up in traffic and late getting home. What a story! It took me a long time to explain it to Marie. "Your *brodo di pesce* is cold," she told me coldly, as though it would never warm up.'

"Marie is Joe's wife," Mr. Rabinowitz explained. "She'd spent most of that day preparing Joe's favorite dish, a fish chowder made from his mother's recipe. Marie was planning to surprise him."

"Yes," said Sam. "But why was he late?"

"I'm just coming to that part," said Sam's father. "It was almost dinnertime. Joe had dropped his last fare for the day. His off-duty sign was turned on. He was on his way home. He hadn't gone more than a block or two when he found himself in a huge traffic jam. Police cars and fire engines were blocking the street. A large crowd of people was still gathering. Everyone was looking up. Joe could tell he wasn't going anywhere for a while. He parked his cab and joined the crowd. He looked up too. He saw a lady perched on the edge of the roof of a very tall building. She was holding something in her hand.

" 'She's going to jump,' said some of the people.

" 'Don't jump, lady,' shouted some of the others.

" 'Go ahead, jump!' One or two encouraged her. Joe watched from the sidelines as the police brought her down.

" 'Jump?' She glared at the police and all the reporters. 'Why would I want to do that?' Then suddenly she understood, and hurriedly explained.

" 'I'm a photographer, an artist,' she told them. 'I specialize in city scenes. My photographs are shown in exhibits. They illustrate books. Some are even hung in museums. I planned this shot for a long time. *City at Dusk from a Rooftop,* I was going to call it. Now you've spoiled it. The light has changed, it's almost dark, a whole day's work has been wasted.' She held up the object in her hand. Everyone could see it was a camera.

"The crowd began dispersing. The police and fire fighters got back into their vehicles and drove off. So did the reporters. Only the woman and Joe were left.

" 'She looked about to cry,' said Joe. 'I took her home in my cab for free. What else could I do? My off-duty sign was already on, and besides, she's an artist like me. Of course, when I offered, I didn't know she lived in New Jersey. "Next time try asking. It's a good thing she didn't live in Alaska," said Marie.' "

Mr. Rabinowitz stopped talking. Abigail and Sam still were eating. Sam chewed fast, and swallowed.

"I thought you said Mr. Sabatini was a dancer."

His father thought a minute, then saw Sam's point. "Sure, a dancer," he answered. "Painter, dancer, photographer, weaver, potter, poet, storyteller, singer, musician, or translator; we're all artists just the same."

"Exactly," said Ms. Rabinowitz, who'd eaten breakfast much earlier, and was now poring over her Russian-English dictionary.

·   ·   ·   ·   ·

Some days later Mr. and Ms. Rabinowitz were getting dressed to go out, to a poetry reading. "We're leaving Abigail in charge. She's older," Ms. Rabinowitz told both children.

"It's so unfair. She'll always be older. I'll never be in charge," Sam complained to Benton. Benton sighed. He was a small dog himself. He understood the problem.

"Should I call you a cab?" asked Abigail.

"Don't be silly. We're taking the subway," her mother answered. Mr. Rabinowitz cleared his throat and glanced at his wife. Then for a minute he studied her carefully.

"We could go by cab if you'd like. Or come back that way. Depending on your hose," Mr. Rabinowitz said.

"I beg your pardon?" said his wife. She thought he'd said "clothes."

"Hose?" said Abigail attentively.

"Yes," replied her father. "It was on account of her hose a very pretty lady took my cab just yesterday." Ms. Rabinowitz sighed. "It's a very short story," said Mr. Rabinowitz. Both children and Benton pricked up their ears. Their father continued his tale.

" 'Just drive a few blocks in any direction,' the very pretty lady told me, climbing into my cab. 'And please, whatever you do, don't turn around,' she added. 'My stockings are falling down. I need to pull them up. Or take them off. Well, I couldn't do it on the street, people would be looking,' she explained. I drove downtown about ten blocks. 'Thank you, that's fine,' she said, paid her fare, and got out."

"Which did she do?" asked Abigail.

"Which what?" said her father.

"Did she pull her stockings up, or take them off?"

"How would I know? Even after she gave me a tip and walked away, I was afraid to look."

"That's all very interesting, but you don't have to worry. That lady was probably wearing panty hose," said Ms. Rabinowitz. "My garters come from Paris, France. A person would never need a cab on their account."

"So, did you take a cab last night, or what?" Abigail asked her mother the following morning.

"She really means, how did your clothes hold up?" said Sam.

"Everything held up fine, except for Daddy's foot," their mother answered. "We took the subway going, but decided we'd walk home. It was your father's idea. 'We could use the exercise,' he told me. We walked for miles. It started raining. Of course, we couldn't find a cab. Your father got a huge blister on his big toe."

"How awful," said Abigail.

"Yes," said her mother. "Fortunately, though, as we were passing Grand Central Station, a woman and her daughter noticed our plight, and offered to share their cab with us. They were about to get in themselves. 'Thank you,' we said, and joined them.

"They had just arrived from Iowa. This was their first trip to New York. It had something to do with the daughter and her horse, but we never found out what. The daughter was too flustered to tell us. 'I still can't believe what I saw,' she said, over and over. Her mother was trying to calm her."

"What did she see?" Sam asked.

"That's what I'm telling you. I'm almost at that part," Sam's mother answered. "The girl and her mother had come by train. It was a very long ride. They both were exhausted. The very first thing the girl did when they got off the train was go look for a rest room. Her mother stayed behind with the luggage. They'd heard stories about New York. The rest room was empty when the girl entered, except for herself and one other person. That person was a very tall, very stout woman, totally naked except for soapsuds. She stood, bent over a sink, bathing herself and shampooing her hair. The girl was so startled, she turned right around and ran back to her mother without ever having used the facilities. 'But darling, only think of that poor woman,' the girl's mother said, hoping to soothe her. 'I'm sure she has a nice tub at home that simply won't drain. Or perhaps there's some problem with the water. What else could she do? Imagine trying to find a plumber who makes house calls at night in New York.' "

"Facilities?" said Abigail, and rolled her eyes at Sam.

"Then what happened?" Sam asked his mother.

"Nothing. By then we were home. We told them good night. They were continuing on to Brooklyn."

Just at that minute, Mr. Rabinowitz hopped into the room, and said, "They did ask, as we were getting out, if we knew of a public rest room they could stop at on their way. Of course, your mother explained the situation: 'If you think finding a plumber at night in New York is hard, you should try finding a rest room you can use in this city anytime.' "

"How is your blister?" Sam asked his father.

"Terrible. If I had to stand at work, I'd have to stay home," his father answered.

That same day, in school, Sam had to write a paragraph on anything. He wrote about work. "Driving a cab for a living has advantages," he wrote. "These are some of them: you get to see the city, you meet interesting people, you can do all your work sitting down, sometimes you hear stories. But if you need to use a toilet, or wash up, it can be a problem."

Mr. Rabinowitz was soaking his toe in a bucket of salt water. Ms. Rabinowitz was reading, and the children were doing homework. Benton was trying to nap. Mr. Rabinowitz was first to break the silence. He said, "A man jumped into my cab today at Broadway and Thirty-third Street. 'Metropolitan Museum, please. I'm going to see the Velázquez.'

" 'Really?' I said. 'I was there last week. You are going to love it.' I turned to look at him as I spoke. Something looked wrong. Then I knew what. The man wore no coat on such a cold day. The clothes he had on were frayed and thin, although very clean. I turned on the meter and turned up the heat. As we rode uptown we discussed Spanish art. He was very well informed for such an underdressed person.

"When we were almost at the museum, he said, 'I'm sorry to have to tell you this, but I have no money to pay the fare. I can tell you a story instead.' Well, what could I do? We were nearly there. I couldn't see putting him out in the cold. I *was* curious how he planned to pay for the museum. I drove, and listened to his story:

'Once a man jumped into a cab and told the driver, "Take me to the Met, please." The driver did. When they were almost there, the man said, "I'm sorry, but I have no money for the fare. I can tell you a story instead. . . ." '

"Just at that minute we arrived at the museum," said Mr. Rabinowitz. "The man in *my* cab opened the door and got out. 'Thank you,' he said. Then he walked to the foot of the entrance steps, removed a narrow case from his pocket, took out a piccolo, and began to play it. People passing paused to listen. Some dropped coins into the open case. I listened too. After some time, the man picked up his coins, packed up his piccolo, climbed the stairs and went into the museum. I picked up a fare heading downtown."

"Your passenger was probably a famous painter down on his luck. That's how he knew so much about art. I'm surprised you didn't see that," said Rita Rabinowitz.

"Maybe he was an art connoisseur," said Abigail, trying out a word she'd heard on public television.

"How can they always miss the point?" Sam asked Benton later that night. The truth was clear to Sam. The man was an out-of-work piccolo player. "If he drove a cab, he could earn enough to buy a coat, and play the piccolo on his days off. Daddy should have told him that," Sam whispered to Benton just before they fell asleep.

# About Barbara Ann Porte

• • • • • • • •

I am a walker myself. I never take a cab. Driving one is out of the question. I spend my life lost. It's also true that trekking miles on foot, even in the stormiest weather, seems less risky to me than turning a key to start a car; or anything else for that matter. It explains why I write in longhand or on a manual typewriter. I should have been a letter carrier. All my best thinking is done out of doors, walking. Still, I can imagine what riding in a cab is like, and why a person might decide to call one. Sagging panty hose and blind guide dogs are not the half of it.

The family in my "taxicab story" first appeared in *Take-Along Dog* (1989) and again in *Taxicab Tales* (1992), both published by Greenwillow Books (a division of William Morrow & Company, Inc.). The children, Abigail and Sam, remind me of a niece and nephew, and are favorite characters of mine. Other of my books include: *Jesse's Ghost and Other Stories*, *I Only Made Up the Roses*, *Ruthann and Her Pig*, and *Fat Fanny, Beanpole Bertha and the Boys*. Some of what happens to the people in my books also happened to me, or to my relatives; or something very similar. The big difference is that what's funny in a story, in real life usually isn't. Writing about it cheers me up.

Not too long ago I moved from New York to Virginia by way of Tennessee. Sometimes I still hunger for Manhattan, where bread is bread, and raisin pumpernickel is generally available. It's too far from here to there to take a cab, and walking is out of the question. Sometimes I write about it.

Adrian tries everything to
get rid of an unwanted itch—
but sometimes sisters know best.

• • • • • • • • • •

# THE ITCH

## Marjorie Weinman Sharmat

**I**n a faraway village there once lived a fat and comfortable boy named Adrian, whose pink and cheery skin hung about him in soft lumps.

Adrian had a fat and comfortable mother, father, sister, and dog.

Adrian, in fact, had everything he wanted.

And more.

In an otherwise perfect life, Adrian had an itch.

Adrian's itch was not an ordinary one. It first appeared at a most inconvenient time, when his family had guests for dinner. In the beginning the itch felt merely like a small tingle under one of the pink lumps in the upper part of Adrian's left arm. Adrian quickly reached over with his right hand and scratched the spot. "So much for that," thought Adrian.

But the itch did not go away.

Again Adrian reached over and scratched. And again and again.

"What a disgusting and presumptuous itch," Adrian muttered to himself. "It arrives uninvited at the dinner table and begs for attention."

Adrian's mother and father were busy talking to their guests. But Adrian's sister, Fudgka, kicked him under the table. "Do not scratch while you eat," she whispered. "Bad manners. Very bad manners."

But Adrian kept scratching.

After the guests left, Adrian went up to his mother and father. "I have a guest too," he said. "I am visited by an itch that will not go away."

"Perhaps it will disappear after a good night's sleep, son," said his mother.

Adrian went to bed. But he was too itchy to sleep. "Help!" he cried.

Adrian's family helped. All through the night his mother and father and Fudgka took turns scratching Adrian's itch.

When the sun rose Adrian said, "My itch is still here to greet the morning. And my left arm has turned from pink to angry red."

Adrian's father plumped the pillows and brought Adrian breakfast in bed. "Your favorite dumplings," he said. "I hope they will make you feel better, my son."

"They will make only my stomach feel better," said Adrian as he ate up all the dumplings.

"Your mother and I have to go visit your grandmother," said Adrian's father. "We will be gone a week. But Fudgka, your fine older sister, will take good care of you and your itch."

Fudgka folded her arms. "Good care, good care." She chuckled.

Adrian's mother and father packed their knapsacks and left.

Adrian stayed in bed and scratched.

"Still scratching?" Fudgka asked four hours later.

"You are supposed to take good care of me," Adrian said. "Get rid of my itch."

"I do not do itches," Fudgka said. "I take care of important things. If this turns into a major disease, I will help."

"Never mind," Adrian said. "I am going out for a walk. Perhaps there is something in this house that makes me itch. Like you."

Adrian got dressed and started to walk to the village square. As he walked he could not keep from scratching his arm. He tried to do it as secretively as possible, but the villagers noticed and heads turned toward him.

"Why," Adrian asked himself, "if I must have an itch at all, does it have to be a conspicuous itch? Why not a timid little itch that can be scratched away under a table? Or a polite little itch that appears only at private times when I can attack it with the proper gusto?"

Adrian could not bear the thought of everyone staring at him. He turned around and went home. He climbed back into bed so that he could scratch in the most comfortable and private position.

News of Adrian's itch spread throughout the village.

The villagers felt great sympathy toward the Boy with the Itch, as they started to call him.

However, there was one boy in the village who, when he heard of Adrian's misfortune, smiled gleefully and rubbed his hands together in anticipation. This boy, named Zonkus, yearned for fame. "I *know* I will grow up to be famous," he thought. "But the sooner, the better. If I can cure Adrian of his itch, everyone will know of me and admire me right now."

Then Zonkus frowned. "There is one minor problem in my scheme. I do not know how to cure an itch. But with my superior intelligence and unlimited ingenuity, I am certain I will think of something."

Zonkus went to Adrian's house and knocked on the door. Adrian did not want to see anyone. But Zonkus called, "Adrian, I am just a boy like you. But I know more than all the villagers put together. I came here not to offer sympathy, but to cure you of your itch."

Adrian leaped out of bed and flung open the door. "A cure?" he exclaimed. "Come in. Come in."

Zonkus walked in.

"You are smaller than I am," Adrian said. "How can *you* help me?"

"Size does not count," Zonkus said. "My head is full of wisdom."

Fudgka was listening. "Your head is full of hair," she said. "And that is all it is full of."

Zonkus turned to Adrian. "I know of a splendid ointment that cured Hickel's pig of her incessant itch."

"Hickel's pig!" exclaimed Fudgka. "That fat pink creature!"

"Do not think of her that way," said Zonkus. "Think only that she is now itchless."

"Bah!" said Fudgka.

"Adrian, we must go to Hickel's house," said Zonkus.

"Do not go, Adrian," said Fudgka.

"I must," said Adrian.

"I will not go with you," said Fudgka. "Your sister Fudgka does not visit pigs."

Adrian and Zonkus went to Hickel's house.

"Hickel," said Zonkus, "we have come for some of your fine ointment to cure Adrian's itch."

"Of course," said Hickel. "Look how my pig Schlusser lies there in the mud, happy and itchless. You should have seen her last week, scratching, scratching."

Hickel brought forth a small jar filled with a yellowish ointment. "Here is my ointment," he said. "It is made of the finest garlic, chicken fat, salt from the sea, and dried leaves."

"Ugh," said Adrian. "Do you think I am the sort of boy who would use such a concoction? Its odor is stronger than that of the slop in the pig's pen."

"Nonsense," said Zonkus as he dipped his finger into the jar and rubbed the ointment on Adrian's left arm. "Observe that happy itchless pig while you are waiting for the ointment to work."

"I do not want to look at an itchless pig," said Adrian as he held his nose and tried not to scratch his arm.

Adrian waited patiently for the ointment to work. But at last he gave up, reached over with his right hand

and vigorously scratched his left arm. "This ointment is a failure," he said sadly.

"No, it is not," said Zonkus. "But perhaps your itch needs something more. Come with me."

Zonkus and Adrian went to Zonkus's house, where Zonkus brought forth five robes. "Here," he said, "is what your itch needs."

"Five robes?" exclaimed Adrian.

"Five robes to be worn at the same time," said Zonkus. "You will become increasingly hot, and you will sweat out your itch."

"Well, perhaps that is better than looking to an itchless pig for hope," said Adrian.

Zonkus helped Adrian put on the robes. First one, then another. And another. And another. And another.

"I am so hot, I will sweat to death!" cried Adrian.

"No," said Zonkus, "the sweat of your body will turn into rivers and oceans of sweat and your itch will drown in them."

"When?" asked Adrian.

"It might take a day or so," said Zonkus.

"A day!" cried Adrian. "I know what will happen. I will die of sweat, and my itch will die also."

"Patience," said Zonkus. "Even at this very moment, your itch is beginning to drown."

Adrian scratched his arm through the five robes. "My itch is alive and well, but I am not," he said. "If I am to drown, I would prefer to do it in the cool waters of the stream."

"Patience," said Zonkus again.

And so Adrian was patient.

When darkness came, Zonkus peered at him and asked, "Why are you still scratching, my friend?"

"Because I am still itching, my friend!" shouted Adrian, and he tore the five robes from his body.

"Do not despair," said Zonkus. "Your itch will go away, I promise."

"How?" asked Adrian.

"Well, now that we have put ointment on your itch and it has had a good sweat, it must be left alone," said Zonkus. "So you must climb to the top of the highest mountain, where your itch can be alone."

"The top of the highest mountain?" exclaimed Adrian. "That will take many days and nights of hard climbing."

"I agree," said Zonkus. "But it is well worth the effort to get rid of your itch. You must start right away. I will wait for you at the bottom of the mountain."

Adrian groaned and began to climb. The night was black and starless, which made the climb slow and difficult, and even worse, Adrian had to stop and scratch his arm every few moments.

Adrian grew hungry. "Now it would be nice to have some of Hickel's ointment," he thought. "To eat. When one is hungry, garlic, chicken fat, salt from the sea, and dried leaves can be a sumptuous feast."

Adrian continued to climb. The night wind blew cold and hard. "Now it would be nice to have one of Zonkus's five robes to keep me warm," he thought. "Perhaps all five."

Adrian climbed for many days and nights. He thought of sweat in order to keep himself warm. To keep from starving, he ate shrubs that he found along the way.

Finally Adrian reached the top of the mountain. He sat down on it. "At last!" he exclaimed. "My itch and I are all alone up here. *Now* it will surely go away."

Adrian waited. But his itch did not go away.

"Itch, there is no one else here," he said. "You are left alone, just as Zonkus instructed. So why are you not going away?"

Adrian stood up. "It is no use. I have climbed for days and nights. I have eaten shrubs and dreamed of sweat. And now I find myself talking to an itch. I am too clever to do this sort of thing. Except that I have already done it."

Adrian climbed down the mountain.

Zonkus was at the bottom, asleep and snoring.

Adrian woke him up. "I itch," said Adrian.

Zonkus was instantly awake.

"You still itch? That is bad news for me."

"For *you*?" Adrian repeated.

Zonkus was thinking, *If I cannot cure his itch, I might have to wait until I am all grown up in order to be famous.*

"Never mind," Zonkus said. "I know that your itch will go away, my friend. But you must do one more thing. You must go and stand in the village square and wave your arm back and forth in the air until the itch flies away. It will leave the center of the village and keep going until it is well out of town and returns to the dark, unfathomable place from where it came."

"I don't know," said Adrian. "The climb to the top of

the mountain took away my strength. How long must I stand and wave?"

"Not more than a week," said Zonkus.

"A week!" cried Adrian.

"Patience," said Zonkus.

Adrian and Zonkus walked to the village square. There Adrian raised his left arm and waved it back and forth, back and forth. Curious villagers gathered around to watch this strange activity. They asked one another, "Why is this boy carrying on so? Has his itch gone to his head?"

Then the word spread of all the things Adrian had done to try to rid himself of his itch, and that this was yet another attempt. The villagers rushed up to Adrian and said, "You are a boy of courage and bold spirit." They wished him good luck, and some brought him small gifts.

But when Fudgka saw him, she cried, "At last I have found you. And I know what you have been up to. Have you forgotten that I am in charge of you? I am in charge, and you are coming home."

Fudgka tugged at Adrian's unwaving right arm.

"I cannot go home," Adrian said. "Zonkus said I must wave and have patience."

Fudgka sighed. "Very well. I will have to take care of you right here in the village square."

Fudgka brushed Adrian's teeth and hair and gave him dumplings and milk and kisses, and went home.

Adrian continued to wave. And scratch.

And Zonkus continued to say, "Your itch will go away, my friend. I promise."

Suddenly Adrian lowered his arm and shouted, "The

itch wins! I lose! I am going home to scratch in privacy."

"No!" shouted Zonkus. "Patience!"

But Adrian rushed home.

Fudgka said, "I told you not to go with Zonkus. Now look at you. Poor Adrian, so tired and dirty. I will give you a nice warm bath."

Adrian sat in the washtub while Fudgka scrubbed him all over. "I will wash off the ointment, the sweat, the mountain dirt, and the village dust," she said.

Fudgka scrubbed away while Adrian scratched. Then all at once he stopped scratching.

*"It is gone!!!"* Adrian shouted. *"My good sister, Fudgka, you have washed and scrubbed away my itch!!"*

"Oh, my good, pink, cheery brother, Adrian," said Fudgka. "How lucky you are to have such a clever sister."

Just then there was a knock on the door. Zonkus walked in. He looked at Adrian, who was happily splashing in the tub.

Zonkus grinned. "Ah, Adrian," he said. "You are not scratching anymore. Your itch has gone. Didn't I, your good friend Zonkus, promise you that your itch would go away? How fortunate that you took my advice and used the ointment and wore the five robes and climbed to the top of the mountain and waved your arm back and forth in the village square!"

Adrian leaped out of the tub and shook his fist at Zonkus.

"Why are you shaking your fist at me?" cried Zonkus

as he turned and ran from the house. Adrian threw on his robe and ran after him.

Zonkus ran through the streets. Adrian was close behind him shouting, "I wish you an itch! I wish you an itch!"

Zonkus ran faster and faster. Adrian ran slower and slower. At last Adrian grew tired and stopped. He went home.

Then he and Fudgka got ready for their mother's and father's return. When their parents got home, they looked first at Adrian. "Your itch?" they asked.

Fudgka answered. "*I* got rid of it," she said proudly. "I took perfect care of Adrian all the time you were gone."

"Good, we will give you that task every time we go away," said her mother.

"Do not be hasty, Mother," said Fudgka.

Adrian's itch never came back. And his life was even better than before. He was greatly admired by everyone in the village and assured of a certain immortality as the brave boy who tried so hard and so long to overcome a most uncommon itch.

Adrian's fame, however, was eventually surpassed by that of Zonkus. Zonkus, in fact, achieved more fame than he wanted and in quite an unexpected way. After he grew up, he was often seen wearing five robes at a time, climbing to the top of the highest mountain, waving his left arm in the village square and staring rather enviously at Hickel's pig.

# About Marjorie Weinman Sharmat

•••••••

I know all about itches. My most persistent one, starting in childhood, was to become a published writer. I've now stopped scratching. I've had over one hundred books published for children and young adults. I've also novelized a CBS-TV sitcom and the movie *Supergirl*.

My books have been published in fourteen languages. Numerous titles have been Junior Literary Guild and Book of the Month Club selections, CBC/IRA Choices, and state award winners and runner-ups. The pilot for the PBS-TV Reading Rainbow series was based on my book *Gila Monsters Meet You at the Airport*. My best-known character is *Nate the Great,* who has been sleuthing since 1972. Nate, who uses his head as well as his feet to solve mysteries, is on permanent display in an exhibit on the brain and learning at the Museum of Science and Industry in Chicago.

"The Itch" is my first story in the folktale genre. It was my chance to engage in broad drama and rampant silliness while zeroing in on little cores of truth about human nature. Gullibility, responsibility, chicanery, trust, and affection . . . rich territory! And siblings in charge . . . is Fudgka the ultimate baby-sitter?

My latest project is the Olivia Sharp, Agent for Secrets series, coauthored with my husband, Mitchell. Titles so far are *The Pizza Monster, The Princess of the Fillmore Street School, The Sly Spy,* and *The Green Toenails Gang*. Our two sons, Craig and Andrew, are also published authors. I suppose that our dog Dudley is too. His "autobiography," immodestly but accurately titled *I'm the Best!* is a 1991 publication.

Monty knows that there is
money to be made everywhere—and that's
exactly what he plans to do.

• • • • • • • • • • •

# MONTY'S BUSINESS

## Zilpha Keatley Snyder

**M**y little brother, Mont-
gomery Ashton, has had this thing about money for
almost his entire life. Ever since he swallowed a dime
while everyone else was eating cake and ice cream at
his third birthday party. They had to rush him to the
hospital, but finally everything came out all right—including the dime. Monty seemed to feel fine afterwards
and the whole thing turned out to be harder on the rest
of the family than it was on him. And embarrassing
too. Particularly when Monty refused to leave the hospital until the doctors gave him his dime back.

Nobody knows where Monty got his money fixation
because there's no way it could be inherited. No one
else in the family has even what you might call a nor-
mal interest in the subject. There are four of us besides

Monty—my dad, who is a minister, my mom, who raises kids and organic vegetables, Farley, who is sixteen and plays the oboe, and me, Amy. I'm thirteen and I'm planning to be something useful and interesting like a librarian or a schoolteacher. I mean, talk about a lot of good ways to barely make a living.

But then there is Monty. My dad says that Monty must be a throwback to some distant ancestor who was a big business tycoon, or else maybe a pirate. But I still think it was the dime that did it. After all, as my mom is always saying, you are what you eat.

Right at first everyone thought it was kind of cute. I mean, when a four-year-old opens up his own business, even if it's only a lemonade stand, everyone is pretty impressed. Especially when they find out he can already count money and make change with deadly accuracy. At the age of four Monty could make change faster than a supermarket checkout clerk, but he couldn't read and write yet, so I got roped into the act. I was only about eight at the time, but I had to print his signs for him.

"Write ten cents, Amy," Monty said, chewing on his lower lip the way he always does when he's figuring about money. "Ten cents for kids. Twenty-five for grown-ups."

"Okay," I said. "Ten for kids and twenty-five . . . How come so much more for grown-ups? Do they get bigger glasses?"

Monty frowned. At four Monty already had these dark, V-shaped eyebrows, and when he frowned they tilted down in the middle over his pug nose, which made him look like a baby vampire. "No," he said, holding up one of the little paper cups from the dispenser in the church's social hall. "Everybody gets these same glasses. All the same."

I stopped printing. "Oh, yeah? Then why do grown-ups have to pay more?"

Monty looked exasperated, as if I'd asked a very silly question. "Because," he said. "Because grown-ups got more money."

I guess that must have seemed like a good argument to me at the time, because I remember writing the signs the way he wanted them. Ten cents for kids. Twenty-five for grown-ups.

Monty didn't get rich selling lemonade. After Mom ran out of lemons and the social hall ran out of cups, he lost interest and went on to a new project. I don't remember which of his businesses came exactly next because there were so many. But it wasn't too much later that he thought up the money-making scheme that came to be known as the Christmas Tree Fiasco.

I think Monty must have been about six at the time, and he should have known better. A six-year-old should have enough sense to know that a tree won't grow without its roots. At least that's what Farley said when he got blamed for not checking on what Monty was doing and making him stop. It was a couple of weeks after Christmas and Dad and Mom had put Farley, who was thirteen at the time, in charge while they went to some kind of afternoon meeting at the church. And while they were gone Monty collected about a half dozen discarded Christmas trees from Dumpsters and trash cans and planted them in our front lawn. Apparently he thought that the trees would start growing again and that he could sell them for lots of money next Christmas, which of course was pretty funny. Except that my dad didn't think the six big holes in his precious front lawn were a very good joke.

Over the years there were a lot more of Monty's "big business" schemes. There was, for instance, a circus held in a tent made of taped-together black garbage bags. The usual thing—lions and tigers. Dogs with crepe-paper manes and our yellow cat with painted-on stripes. And a fairly funny clown—Monty, himself, in a kitchen mop wig and a Ping-Pong-ball nose.

And just a couple of years ago there was his pet baptismal service, when he convinced most of his second-grade classmates to pay him fifty cents to have their pets baptized in the church's marble baptismal font. He'd conducted ceremonies for several dogs, a cat, a hamster, and a nanny goat before Dad found out and made him stop. He'd scheduled all the baptisms for when Dad was away visiting shut-ins, but it turned out the goat wasn't housebroken (or in this case churchbroken) and it left some clues in the baptismal alcove that kind of—well, you might say—spilled the beans.

I guess my dad would say that the pet baptisms and the Christmas-tree plantation were Monty's worst ideas, but I'm sure my mom would say it was the rats.

Monty's rat farm started just last year, when he was in third grade. His teacher, Ms. Farrow, had a health-and-nutrition project in which the class fed white rats different diets to see how the foods they ate affected their growth and health. Of course, when the project was over, the rat that got candy and cola and potato chips and stuff like that was small and grungy-looking, and the one that got vegetables and whole grains was big and sleek. But then Ms. Farrow, who didn't like rats very much, gave them away to the member of the class who wrote the best essay on the rat experiment. Guess who won?

At our house both the rats lived in one cage, and of course, they both ate lots of good organic stuff from Mom's garden. Before long Skinny Rat got as fat and sassy as Fat Rat. And after a few weeks Skinny Rat got even fatter—temporarily. Monty sold the first batch of babies to his friends for three dollars apiece, and that got him really excited.

"I'm going to make a lot of money in the rat business," he said at dinner one night. "Raising rats is a smart way to make money." He looked at Farley. "A lot smarter than mowing lawns or washing cars." Farley did lawns and cars sometimes when he needed extra cash.

Farley sneered. Besides being a major genius on the oboe and a world authority on any subject you might care to mention, Farley is a world-class sneerer. "Yeah," he said. "Very smart. Until you run out of friends to sell them to. Or until we get raided by the Environmental Protection Agency." He looked at Mom and Dad. "Have you tried breathing at our end of the hall lately?" He held his nose and pretended he was passing out.

Mom looked worried, and a couple of days later Monty had to move his rat farm out into the garage. But that didn't solve all the problems. Just as Farley had predicted, Monty began to run out of customers, and at one point he left a cage door open and about a dozen half-grown rats escaped and started roaming around the neighborhood. And Mrs. Hurley, our next-door neighbor, who has a real problem where rats are concerned, started having daily screaming fits in her backyard.

That was the beginning of the end, and before long Dad rounded up all the rats—there must have been around fifty by then—and took them away. He wouldn't say where to, and I preferred not to think about it. I'm not particularly crazy about rats, but I'd gotten rather fond of old Fat and Skinny. But Monty didn't even seem to mind. By then he had some other "multimillion-dollar" scheme on his mind.

But as far as causing really serious problems goes, none of Monty's businesses came even close to what happened just last month, at the white elephant sale.

The church's white elephant sale is held every year, and the money is donated to some extraworthy cause, like the homeless or the World Food Bank. The sale always starts on a Thursday and last three days. All the Sunday school kids are supposed to help by going around the neighborhood getting people to donate things for the sale, and in other ways too. My job was to help old Mrs. Hurley put the price labels on everything on Wednesday evening. And Monty, because he is such a whiz with money, was supposed to be in charge of the sales desk on Thursday and Friday afternoon and all day on Saturday. But on Friday morning when Mom was setting up the sales desk, she noticed that something terrible had happened. The rest of the family heard about it that evening.

Mom had been very quiet during dinner. I kind of wondered about it because she generally holds up her end of a conversation better than average. Dad must have wondered, too, because once he asked her if everything was all right. She said it was, but then, after Monty had gone off to watch his favorite TV program, she told the rest of us what had happened. Someone had stolen over fifty dollars from the Thursday sales.

"Stolen?" Dad said. "But when? And how? Wasn't it locked in the storage room last night?"

Mom nodded. The church didn't have a real cash register, so during the day the money was kept in the sales desk, but at the end of each day, Mom always put the money away on a shelf in the storage room at the bottom of the bell tower—and locked the door.

"Did you count it before you locked up?" Dad asked.

"Yes, of course," Mom said. "I counted it. There was seventy-three dollars in bills and nine-something in change. Monty counted it, too, and then he helped me take it into the tower storage room."

"You're sure you locked the door?" Dad asked.

Mom nodded slowly. "I watched. Monty locked it."

I looked at Mom and then at Dad. They were looking at each other and their faces looked stiff and painful.

"I knew it," Farley said. "I knew that kid was going to end up in jail."

Mom's face looked like it was going to fall apart.

"Good old Farley," I said. "You can always count on old Farley to make the worst of everything. We don't *know* that Monty took it."

"Amy's right," Dad said. "And besides, in spite of

Monty's fondness for filthy lucre, he's never done anything before that was actually illegal."

"Oh, yeah?" Farley said. "How about counterfeiting? How about that time I caught him in the church office photocopying the ten dollar bill he got for his birthday?"

"Oh, Farley," Mom said. "That wasn't counterfeiting. He was just making toy money to play grocery store with."

Farley sneered. "Yeah, that's what he *said* he was doing."

"To get back to the problem at hand," Dad said. "Someone else could have broken in during the night. Was the door still locked this morning?"

Mom nodded.

"And was anything else disturbed or missing?"

"Not that I noticed. The lid was off the shoe box I'd put the paper money in. But nothing else seemed to have been touched."

"Have you mentioned the missing money to Monty?"

Mom shook her head. "Not yet."

After that Mom and Dad decided she should tell Monty about the missing money before he went to bed that night. Just to see what he would say. Not as if he were suspected or anything, but just as if to ask his help in trying to figure out what might have happened.

That was pretty much the end of our conference, and a little later I went to bed feeling upset and worried. I kept picturing all sorts of horrible things, like newspaper headlines saying MINISTER'S NINE-YEAR-OLD SON ARRESTED FOR ROBBERY. I couldn't get to sleep and I was still awake a little before midnight when I heard

someone tiptoeing past my door and down the stairs.
Of course, it was Monty.

I put on my slippers and followed him, close enough
to see that he was carrying a flashlight and wearing his
robe and unlaced Nikes. He went down the stairs and
right into Dad's study. I stood outside the door and
heard a drawer opening and then the jingle of keys. A
solid, heavy jingle like the big ring of church keys that
Dad always keeps in his top drawer. I ducked back
behind the corner as he came out of the study and
went down the hall to the back door.

Outside, he headed directly across the parking lot
and on into the church. I took a minute to grab Dad's
old raincoat off the hook on the back porch and slip it
on over my pajamas before I followed.

There was no problem getting in the church. Monty
had left one of the big front doors a little bit open.
Inside the vestibule I noticed right away that the door
to the bell tower was open, too, and the light was on.
No one was in sight, but I could hear some scuffling
noises coming from inside the tower. I tiptoed to the
door and peeked in.

The bell tower is actually just a tall, narrow, four-
sided building about three stories high. At ground level
it is a small room, empty except for the hanging bell
ropes and some shelves Dad built around the walls to
hold church supplies. A ladder attached to one wall
leads up to a floor just below the bells. Actually it's not
so much a floor as a platform, with a big hole in the
middle so the ropes can hang down.

All of us kids had helped Dad ring the church bells
from time to time, but we'd always been forbidden to

climb up the ladder, because of the dangerous open hole in the middle of the platform. But when I got to the door Monty was already nearly to the top of the ladder. I must have gasped or something because he immediately looked down and saw me.

"Oh. Hi, Amy," he said over his shoulder and went on climbing. "Wait a minute. I think I found out . . ."

But then he disappeared onto the platform. He was still talking, but I couldn't make out what he was saying. I didn't hear anything else clearly until he shouted, "Yeah! I found it. Look out. There she goes."

There were more scuffling noises and then he yelled again, only this time it was more of a scream, and then both of his legs came through the hole in the platform. For a second or two they thrashed around and both his Nikes came off and crashed down in front of me. I'd started to run to the ladder when the rest of him came through the hole. I watched him fall. It seemed to take a long, long time before he hit the floor and lay still.

Monty's arm was broken, and his left ankle, but the worst part was that he was unconscious for quite a long time. And when he finally did come to, he seemed different. He spoke slowly and carefully and asked strange questions, like where he was and if it was still August, and he didn't seem to remember anything at all about the accident. There was a stiffness about his face and nothing you could say or do would make him smile.

We all stayed at the hospital most of the next day, but in the afternoon Dad drove Farley and me home. He spent some time calling people and taking care of church business and then he went back to the hospital. I stayed in my room for a while thinking about the scared and puzzled look in Monty's eyes when he asked what month it was.

And thinking about how Mom kept telling him he was all right and that he'd remember everything before long, and then how she went out into the hall and stood for a long time with her head leaning back against the wall with a still, calm expression on her face except for the frightened look in her eyes. And then I thought of something else and I got up and dried my eyes and went over to the church.

Mrs. Hurley was there arranging flowers and she let me in. I had to answer a lot of questions before she went back to the flowers and let me alone. But as soon as she did I went to the tower room, and I hadn't been more than a few minutes when I'd solved the entire mystery.

On the shelf right near the money box I noticed something only too familiar—rat droppings. So I climbed up the ladder, and on the platform below the bells, tucked away in a dark corner, I found nine brand-new baby rats in a cozy nest made out of greenbacks—ones and fives and even a twenty or two. So then I climbed quickly, but *very* carefully, back down the ladder and got my bike and rode to the hospital.

When I was almost to Monty's room I saw Mom and Dad walking down the hall with Dr. Brawley, but before they saw me they all went into the doctor's office. I guessed they were having some kind of a conference, so I waited a little while outside the door and then I went on up to Monty's room.

He seemed to be asleep when I first walked in, but after a while he opened his eyes and looked at me, but he didn't say anything. He was frowning but in a strange dull way, instead of with his fierce baby-vampire glare. He didn't answer when I said "Hi," so I just started talking.

First I told him all about what I'd found in the bell tower—about the nest full of money and the nine baby rats and everything. And then, when he still didn't say anything, I said, "I'll bet you saw some rat droppings on Thursday evening when you and Mom were putting the money away and locking up. You probably didn't say anything right then because you figured it was one of your rats that escaped that time. And you knew Mom wouldn't be too pleased to hear there was a rat living in the church. But then, as soon as she told you about the missing money, you must have guessed. About what the rat had done, I mean, because of the way they used to love to make nests for their babies out of paper napkins and towels and stuff like that. And I'll bet the mother rat was up there when you climbed up and maybe you tried to catch her or something and that's how you happened to fall. Was that how it was?"

Monty didn't answer. He went on staring at me without saying anything, but just then the door opened and Mom and Dad and Dr. Brawley came in. They all said hello to me and asked me how I got back to the hospital, and things like that, and then they all looked at Monty.

But Monty was still looking at me. "Nine?" he asked all of a sudden, and when I nodded he nodded back very slowly and started chewing on his lower lip. After a few seconds he grinned, kind of lopsided and wobbly, as if he'd just remembered how. "Twenty-seven dollars," he said.

"What?" everyone said. "What is it, Monty?"

Monty went on looking at me and when he started to say, "Nine times three dollars is twenty-seven," I said it, too, in unison.

Mom and Dad and the doctor were still looking blank and worried when I jumped up and started dancing around the room.

"Amy," Dad said. "Stop that. What are you doing?"

I stopped dancing, but I couldn't stop grinning. "It's okay." I said. "Everything's okay. Monty's back in business."

# About Zilpha Keatley Snyder

. . . . . . . .

I was born and raised in rural California, where a passion for books and reading led me to declare myself a writer at the age of eight. It wasn't until I was about to graduate from college that my determination to write or starve wavered enough to allow me to prepare myself to become a teacher. Although it was my second choice as a profession I learned to enjoy teaching, and my years in the classroom led to a deep admiration for and fascination with people in the middle and upper years of childhood. So after about ten years devoted almost exclusively to teaching and to my own growing family, I came back to writing—this time for young people.

I now live in Mill Valley, California, with my husband, Larry, who is a professor of music at Sonoma State University. Our three children are grown and away from home.

Like so many of my stories, "Monty's Business" has one root that goes back to my own childhood, when I happened to have a young neighbor who was quite like Monty. I distinctly remember the day he showed up at our back door, selling paper napkins which, he announced proudly, had been "hardly used at all." I was quite young myself at the time, but I recall thinking that our enterprising young neighbor was a real character. And now he has become one.

. . . . .

Zilpha Keatley Snyder has received Newbery Honor Book awards three times: for *The Egypt Game, The Headless Cupid,* and *The Witches of Worm.* Her most

## ABOUT ZILPHA KEATLEY SNYDER

recent books are *Libby on Wednesday,* which tells of the effect that a writing workshop has on a group of children, and *The Song of the Gargoyle,* a fantasy about the son of a court jester, who travels on his own through medieval Europe when his father is kidnapped. She is currently working on a contemporary adventure in which some teenagers explore an old gold mine.

When flower girls Mokie the klutz
and Brittany the princess have to
walk down the aisle side by side,
anything might happen . . . and it does.

• • • • • • • • • • •

# WEDDING FEVER

## Jan Greenberg

**"T**he whole thing's out of
control," said Mokie Mosby, slurping down orange
juice. "Even poor Nerdy's acting weird."

"If you're referring to my future husband, it's *Neddy,*
thank you very much. And he's as happy as I am about
having a big wedding," retorted her sister Mae, who
sat at the table writing thank-you notes.

"Then why is he always muttering to himself?"
asked Mokie. " 'Specially around me."

"Maybe if you'd stop making frog faces and calling
him Nerdy . . ."

Mokie pulled her mouth lopsided, which usually
made Mae laugh. But this time Mae rolled her eyes and
turned away. Mokie sighed. Her sister was much more
fun before she met Nerdy.

For months Mae and her mother talked nonstop about the wedding, going over every minute detail a hundred times. She and her father had been pushed aside, discarded like old rags in favor of monogrammed towels, new bed linens, and embroidered tablecloths.

Mae slapped her notes into efficient little piles. They covered the table like a hand of solitaire, leaving Mokie no place to eat. She stomped around the room waving her toast.

"It's babyish to be a flower girl. Why can't I be a bridesmaid instead?"

"Because you're only eleven, Margaret darling. That's why," said Mae firmly. "Trust me. This is the way it's supposed to be."

Mae always seemed to know how things were supposed to be, as if life were a recipe to be followed, step by step. Mokie preferred making up the ingredients as she went along. With a disgusted snort, she sat down, missing the chair, knocking into the table, and landed with a thud on the floor. Mae's notes scattered down on her head.

"I swear," cried Mae, snatching them up, "sometimes I think you do these things on purpose. Nobody could be such a klutz without trying."

"Why are you sprawled on the floor, dear?" asked Mrs. Mosby, carrying in an armload of gifts.

"Don't ask," said Mae. "It's her two left feet again."

"Maybe I'll just skip the wedding and go to Alaska," said Mokie.

"Now, now," said her mother. "What would we do with your flower-girl dress if you go to Alaska?"

"I'm not wearing that frilly thing," said Mokie. "It makes me look like Little Bo Peep!" Yards of net, and underneath, ruffled pantaloons. All she needed was a staff and a flock of sheep. Maybe she should throw a tantrum or pretend to be sick. But it wouldn't work to threaten Mae, who knew all her tricks. Besides, she'd never been to a wedding before. Her father kept referring to it as "the extravaganza." That word reminded Mokie of a circus. She imagined clowns and acrobats tumbling down the aisle, hotdogs and cotton candy for dinner, the bride and groom sailing off in a hot-air balloon.

"Just wait till it's my turn. I'll have a circus," said Mokie. "No dresses allowed—" But her protests were interrupted by loud banging on the back door. In rushed Neddy Perkins, flailing his arms and blustering. His cheeks puffed out like a blowfish, as if he were ready to explode.

"I can't believe this! I made hotel reservations for my relatives months ago," he cried. "And now two weeks before the wedding, the Ritz says they're overbooked. A Shriners' convention or something. Where will we put them all?"

"How many are coming?" asked Mr. Mosby, walking in clutching a stack of bills.

"Oh, about fifty," answered Mae.

"Fifty relatives? You must be kidding," her father said, pretending to pass out. Mokie laughed, but Neddy paced back and forth, muttering to himself.

"Sit down, Neddy," said Mrs. Mosby, "and have a nice hot cup of tea." Tea was her cure for everything.

"We'll just reserve another hotel," Mae said calmly.

But Mokie could tell she was worried, because her left eye started twitching. Whenever her sister got nervous, her eyes twitched. One Halloween Mokie turned Mae's black-net prom dress into an Oreo-cookie costume, and Mae blinked for hours.

Mae scanned the Yellow Pages while Neddy dialed every hotel in town. Finally they managed to find rooms for all but three people: Neddy's sister, Lucy, her husband, Dave, and their daughter, Brittany, from Detroit.

"Let them stay here," suggested Mr. Mosby. "We have plenty of room."

"What a great idea," agreed Mae. Mokie thought sleeping bags in the backyard was a better idea, but her father looked so proud of himself, she kept quiet.

"Well, now that I've solved that crisis, I can go to the office," said Mr. Mosby. "Someone has to pay these wedding bills." And off he went, whistling "Here Comes the Bride." Mrs. Mosby wandered out with the same boxes she'd carried in. Am I the only sane person left around here? thought Mokie.

Mae turned to her sister. "You'll need to straighten your room for Brittany."

"She'll have to sleep somewhere else," said Mokie. "I'm already using the other bed." That was where she piled her books, dirty clothes, and anything else she couldn't stuff in a drawer. It might take days to clean it off.

"You and Brittany have a lot in common," said Neddy brightly. Mokie gave him a dubious look. "Well —you're both the same age."

"Besides that and breathing, name one other thing," said Mokie.

"Now, Margaret, darling," said Mae sweetly, although Mokie knew she wanted to clobber her, "be reasonable. Brittany is my future niece."

Mokie pictured a girl with long floppy ears like the Shermans' Brittany spaniel, Max, across the street. "Why is she named after a dog, anyway?"

"She was born in France," said Neddy. "In Brittany, which is a French province."

"Oh, great! I'll bet she's stuck-up too."

"I'll make a deal with you," said Neddy in a reasonable tone. "If you let Brittany bunk with you, we'll take you to Six Flags as soon as we get back from our honeymoon."

"Can I go on the roller coaster as many times as I want?"

"Now, listen here," Neddy protested, but Mae gave him a look. "Okay. Okay."

"Then it's a deal," said Mokie, grinning. Getting her way always improved her disposition.

"Bribery does it every time," Neddy said.

"Oh, Neddy," said Mae, "you're going to make a wonderful father." Mokie peered over at him. She imagined their children, a row of little Nerdys with beady eyes and blowfish cheeks. Poor Mae, how could she leave their nice family for him?

"Listen," said Neddy. "I've got a brainstorm! Why don't you ask Brittany to be a flower girl too? My sister would be thrilled."

"Of course," agreed Mae. "Why didn't I think of it? Two flower girls will be better than one." Neddy nodded, regarding Mae with approval. This new plan was a definite improvement over the old one.

"So what do you think, Mokie?" asked Mae. "Now you won't have to go down the aisle by yourself."

Mokie didn't answer. Her good mood dissolved as quickly as a puff of smoke. Even though she'd complained about being a flower girl, secretly she was excited to march down the aisle right before Mae and her father. That made her special. But now they'd ruined everything. Suddenly, a dark and terrible thought came into her head. All at once she wished that on the day of Mae's wedding, an earthquake would come and swallow up the whole bridal party—Nerdy, the bridesmaids, and especially Brittany—all slipping through the cracks, never to be heard from again.

The week before the wedding it rained every day. Mokie perched on the window ledge and watched the downpour with satisfaction. Five men from Tent Event hauled an enormous piece of white canvas across the lawn.

"It's a sea of mud out there," Mokie said to her mother. "You need a boat, not a tent." Mae came into the kitchen carrying a big white box.

"Not another present?" groaned Mokie.

"Here, rip it open," Mae told her. "I know you want to."

Peeling away the wrapping paper, Mokie pulled out something small and heavy—a clear glass animal about four inches high. "Look at this!" she gasped. Although she poked fun at the wedding, the presents were hard to dismiss. Mae had received enough stuff to fill a department store. Mokie couldn't get too excited about a bunch of dishes and silver trays. But this glass animal took her breath away.

She turned it over in her hands. "Why, it's a cat! That's what it is!" The label read "Lead crystal. Handcut in France."

Mae read the card. "Love, Lucy, Dave, and Brittany." Mokie's face fell. She had built a wooden wastebasket for Mae at summer camp. It looked almost professional, except for the shellac that ran in little lumps down the side. But how could a wastebasket from Camp Chickagami compare to a lead crystal cat made in France?

As if on cue, Neddy lurched in lugging suitcases. Following him came two rather ordinary-looking people. The woman with a round, chubby face looked just like Neddy. But pausing at the back door stood a tall girl with silky black hair and porcelain skin. She reminded Mokie of a china doll, the kind that sits on the top shelf of the toy store so kids can't touch it. Brittany didn't resemble the Shermans' dog at all.

"Come in and meet everybody," said Neddy. Brittany went around the kitchen, offering her hand to the adults, bending at the knees into a quick curtsy. She sailed by Mokie without a word.

"Nice to meet you too," said Mokie.

Soon everyone was chattering away like old friends, except for Brittany and Mokie. They remained on opposite sides of the kitchen, eyeing each other. Mokie tried to appear aloof. She tilted her chin in the air, sniffing disdainfully every now and then.

"Margaret, I hope you're not coming down with a

cold," said Mrs. Mosby. "Why don't you take Brittany up to your room and help her unpack."

"Here, carry her suitcase," said Neddy.

"Naturally, it's gigantic," murmured Mokie. She dragged it across the linoleum to the back stairs. "You'd better help. This thing weighs a ton," she said as Brittany sashayed past her. Mokie started up the stairs first, moving backward with Brittany holding the other end. They pulled and shoved.

"What's in here?" asked Mokie. "Bricks?"

"Just be careful," ordered Brittany. The suitcase thumped and bumped. Finally, just as they reached the top, Mokie missed a step. "Whoops," she yelped, losing her balance. As she grabbed the banister, she dropped the suitcase. It tottered for a moment on the edge of the step, but Brittany couldn't hold on to it. Down it went, clattering all the way. By the time the suitcase reached bottom, all the contents had spilled out—dresses, shoes, underwear, nightgown—strewn every which way in tangled heaps. And from the banister waved a lacy bra. Mokie didn't know anyone her age who wore a bra yet.

Flustered, she stood there staring. But Brittany flew into action, clambering down to get her suitcase. "My stuff better not be ruined." She grabbed her bra and shook it in Mokie's direction. She gathered the rest of her belongings, examining each item for flaws. Then folding two dresses over her arm, she swished upstairs, leaving Mokie to retrieve the rest.

"Now what?" came Mae's voice from the kitchen.

"I didn't do it on purpose," Mokie said.

"I'll bet," yelled Brittany. "I'd rather spend the weekend with an orangutan."

She surveyed Mokie's room as if she'd been assigned to the dungeon. After showing Brittany where to put her things, Mokie made a quick getaway. First she hid out in the treehouse, watching the men put up the huge tent. Now she understood why they asked Brittany to be a flower girl. Mae wanted her wedding to be perfect, and Brittany, tiptoeing along like a dainty princess, would be perfect. I'll stick out like a sore thumb, she thought, feeling panicky. What if I trip going down the aisle?

After a while she wandered over to the Shermans' and played with Max until it was almost time for the rehearsal dinner. Back in her room, there was no sign of Brittany. Her clothes hung neatly in the closet, her tiny shoes lined in a row on the floor. Next to Brittany in her lacy bra and tiny satin slippers, she would look like a flat-chested baby with big feet.

At the church, Mrs. Honeywell, the wedding consultant, blew her silver whistle and signaled the organist, Mr. Tooney, to play some marching music. "Line up. Mother of the groom first. Bride and her father last." The ten bridesmaids and groomsmen stood in clusters getting to know each other, and paid no attention to Mrs. Honeywell.

"Line up," she commanded. "We'll practice until I see a definite improvement."

After much general confusion and switching places, Mokie found herself next to Brittany, behind Mae's best friends Libby and Paula. Mrs. Honeywell handed Mokie and Brittany baskets filled with fake rose petals. "Float slowly down the aisle and sprinkle lightly as you go." She patted Brittany on the head and poked Mokie in the ribs. "Your turn. Now move out," she barked, as if she were directing a military drill.

Think float, Mokie instructed herself, not flop. It seemed longer than a mile from the back pew to the altar. With every step, she felt her feet getting heavier and heavier, as if the bottom of her shoes were spread with glue. Brittany glided in second position, her toes pointed out like a ballerina.

"Sprinkle those petals," called Mrs. Honeywell.

Brittany tossed her petals one at a time. They fell softly like snowflakes. Mokie threw a big handful. The petals landed in a clump on the floor. Halfway down the aisle, she ran out.

"You with the frizzy hair, take it easy on the petals," boomed Mrs. Honeywell, blowing her whistle. Only a few more steps, Mokie thought. So far so good. The bridesmaids came closer and closer into focus. Finally, the two girls reached the end of the long aisle.

"Split up and position yourselves on either side of the railing," ordered Mrs. Honeywell. Mokie climbed the steps carefully to stand in front of Paula.

I made it, Mokie said to herself, letting out a huge sigh of relief. But what came out wasn't a sigh at all. It was a loud, gulping hiccup. And once she started, she couldn't stop. The more she tried, the louder she hiccuped. Paula slapped her on the back so hard, Mokie fell off the platform, pulling Libby with her. "Definitely not an improvement," screamed Mrs. Honeywell. Everyone started running around to get back to their places. But it was too late. Mae's eye started twitching.

Neddy's cheeks puffed out. And Mrs. Honeywell left in disgust for another wedding rehearsal.

Later that night, Mokie and Brittany undressed in silence. Brittany slipped into bed so carefully that she barely rearranged the covers. "Good night, Margaret," said Brittany, stretching out her name. Mokie made frog faces in the dark. But it didn't make her feel better. She tried to think of the worst thing that ever happened to her. Maybe it was playing the wrong end of the donkey in the Christmas pageant. That was pretty awful. But tonight was even worse. Mae and Neddy hardly spoke to her at dinner. She sat through five courses without taking a bite. No more disasters, she whispered to the ceiling.

"I know how you feel," came Brittany's voice from the other bed.

"How could you know?" asked Mokie.

"I was once a sugar plum in the *Nutcracker* suite."

Mokie remembered seeing it with her grandmother. The sugar plums were a bunch of little kids in purple who bobbed around the stage while a lady with wings did some fancy turns.

"What happened?" She couldn't imagine Brittany doing anything dumb.

"I got scared and threw up all over the stage."

"Really? How gross!" Gross and wonderful! Somehow this new image of Miss Perfect cheered her considerably.

"The other kids called me the puking sugar plum for months."

"You should have heard what they called me after the Christmas pageant!"

"Those flower-girl dresses remind me of my costume," continued Brittany. "They're so poufy, I feel like a cream puff."

Mokie bolted up and switched on the light. "You hate them too?"

"Maybe if we pulled off a few layers," said Brittany. "What do you think?" With that they both scrambled out of bed and into the closet. Soon the floor was littered with scraps of net.

"Much better," said Mokie, stuffing the dresses back on hangers. "No one will know the difference."

"We should get up early and practice," Brittany said, yawning. "Mrs. Honeywell expects a definite improvement."

"I already know how to walk," said Mokie. Soon Brittany was breathing in steady, regular beats. But Mokie squirmed restlessly under the covers, until her eyes became heavy and she drifted off to sleep. She dreamed she was on a long, narrow obstacle course filled with land mines.

The next morning, Mokie awakened all tangled in her sheets. She went to the window and looked out. The sun beamed down from a clear blue sky. The lawn spread before her, lush as a velvet carpet. Beyond the house rose the white tent, like some magical vision from the *Arabian Nights*. A perfect day for the wedding! Mokie felt a surge of relief. At least she had no control over the weather. But as the day wore on Mokie became more and more nervous. A million things could go wrong. Unexpected earthquakes and flash floods, fires or tornados. Most of all she worried about slipping, tripping, stumbling, falling, tumbling, and finally, plummeting down the aisle like a human avalanche.

The bridesmaids wore dresses the color of Pepto-Bismol. They moved so slowly, Mokie thought they'd never get down the aisle. At the altar Neddy and his groomsmen stood at attention. They wore identical penguin suits. As the organ blasted away, a large lady with a hankerchief in her bosom sang "Oh Promise Me." When Mr. Tooney revved up the beat, Mokie knew it was time. At her side shimmered Brittany, tall and resplendent in the filmy dress. Next to Brittany, Mokie felt like a white cupcake. She looked down at her big feet, protruding from the hem of the skirt. Without those extra layers, the skirt drooped unevenly. Mokie's skin itched from the starched ruffles, and the puffy sleeve didn't quite cover the bandage on her elbow.

"Now," cried Mrs. Honeywell. "Now!" As Mokie and Brittany stepped forward, there was a strange ripping noise. They stopped. The noise stopped too.

Mrs. Honeywell prodded them with her whistle. They took two more steps. Something felt funny around Mokie's ankles. The girls exchanged glances; then they looked down. Last night's operation had developed major side effects. The remaining layers of tulle were unraveling bit by bit, yards of net trailing into two heaps on the aisle. Mr. Tooney pounded on the organ, repeating the chords over and over. People turned in their seats to see what was going on.

There was only one thing left to do. Mokie looked up at the rose window and prayed it would work. She grabbed what was left of the skirt and tugged it off, exposing the ruffled pantaloons. Brittany did the same. Together they took off toward the blur of black and pink. Every now and then they halted, hitched up their sagging pantaloons, and threw a few petals. Finally they turned the baskets over, dumped the rest of the petals and made a quick beeline for the altar.

When they reached the railing, instead of separating, Brittany stuck to Mokie like a burr. They turned to face the audience. Mrs. Perkins looked ready to faint. But other people were nodding and smiling as if they'd just done something wonderful . . . when in fact they were standing there in front of God and everyone in their underwear. "Look at those adorable pants outfits," said a lady on the aisle.

If there were any titters, Mr. Tooney drowned them out with the *Wedding March.* Everyone stood up and Mae, resting on her father's arm, came floating down the aisle. Expertly Mr. Mosby steered her right over the puddles of tulle. Mokie and Brittany hid behind the bridesmaids. Huddled together, they shook with laughter, holding their hands over their mouths to block the sound.

"Well, at least I didn't trip," sputtered Mokie.

"And I didn't throw up," said Brittany.

"A definite improvement," they both whispered.

# About Jan Greenberg

• • • • • • • •

I'm a storyteller who likes books with a beginning, a middle, and an end. When I write, I see the tree-lined streets of my childhood. I hear the voice of my mother calling me home for dinner. I smell the wisteria growing under our white picket fence, as well as the odor of my first science experiment. My writing comes from these contrasting memories.

All of my books are autobiographical, from my first novel, *A Season In-Between,* the story of a young girl who faces the death of her father, to my most recent novel, *Just the Two of Us,* the adventures of two best friends in New York City. However, I'm not attempting to recreate a situation exactly as it happened. The advantage of writing fiction is that you can exaggerate, embellish, and expand on a real experience. That's where the creative fun begins.

The idea for "Wedding Fever" was inspired by my oldest daughter's wedding. Some hilarious things happened that I enjoyed turning into fiction. When you think about Mokie Mosby, you will see that my characters aren't tidy, perfect children who behave like the Brady Bunch. They fall more into the Dennis the Menace category. Sometimes, I get in trouble with my daughters, who tell me I'm stealing their best material. That's what happens, I tell them, if you have a mother who's a writer.

At the end of a novel I'd rather have my characters walk out of a snowstorm than into one. In *No Dragons to Slay,* an ALA Best Book in 1984, I wanted to tell the story of a boy who goes through a traumatic illness and not only survives but triumphs over it.

## ABOUT JAN GREENBERG

My latest book is nonfiction, entitled *The Painter's Eye: Learning to Look at Contemporary Art.* Now I'm working on a book about sculpture. My husband and I began collecting contemporary art twenty-five years ago. Later we opened an art gallery, now a center for new American artists. So you see, whether I'm writing fiction or nonfiction, I always incorporate my life into my work.

# THAT'S WHAT FRIENDS ARE FOR

Halloween pranks can be funny—but
don't ever try to trick a ghost.

• • • • • • • • • •

# TRIPLE ANCHOVIES

## Marion Dane Bauer

**"I** want to order a pizza," I
said into the telephone, letting my voice quaver a little
so I would sound like an old lady. "The biggest you've
got."

Kim was across from me, one hand over her mouth,
practically choking on giggles.

"Yeah . . . the extra large," I agreed. "That'll be
fine." I gave Kim a dirty look. If she started me giggling,
too, the guy taking the order was sure to get suspicious. After all, I don't suppose we were the first kids
on earth to think of ordering a pizza and having it sent
to somebody else, someone who wouldn't expect it.
We may have been the first to think of doing it on Halloween, though, and having it sent to Miss Dawson, the
most ancient old lady in town, if not the universe.

Why, she was so old she had probably been born before pizzas were invented!

"And I want green peppers on it," I said, "and onions and mushrooms. Lots of mushrooms."

Kim made a face. She *hated* mushrooms, but then she knew I hated green peppers and onions, for that matter. "Anchovies, Heather," she whispered. "Anchovies too!"

I turned so I couldn't see Kim's face—I didn't want to take a chance of her making me laugh out loud—and added, my voice even more wavery than before, "And don't forget the anchovies, young man. I want triple anchovies."

Behind me I could hear Kim fall out of her chair and roll on the floor, snorting and choking. I suppose it was the "young man" that got to her . . . or the very mention of those dark, salty little blobs of fish neither one of us could abide. But of course, we weren't the ones who were going to have to eat *this* concoction.

It wasn't that we had anything against Miss Dawson, you understand. It was just that our mothers had decided we were too old for trick-or-treating this year, though how you can be the right age for something one time and "too old" just twelve months later is beyond me. So we had been at my house handing out candy all evening, some of it to kids our own age or even older. And I guess we were feeling pretty mean.

Anyway, Miss Dawson came to mind because she lives on the corner of my block and because . . . well, not for any particular reason, really. We just needed to do something. Nothing that would hurt anyone, you understand, or get us into trouble, either. And I suppose we figured Miss Dawson was so old, she wouldn't even realize someone was playing a trick on her. She would probably think it was Meals on Wheels, a bit late in the day. Or a friendly gift from her neighbors. Which it was . . . kind of.

I hung up the phone and turned to Kim, who was lying limply on the floor, hiccuping giggles. "The next step in Operation Pizza," I told her, "is to set up a watch at Miss Dawson's house. We want to be there when she gets her first whiff of piping-hot anchovies!"

The bare lilac bushes along the edge of Miss Dawson's yard didn't hide much, but we crouched behind them anyway. The last trick-or-treaters trailing by on the street didn't bother to turn into Miss Dawson's walk. She had her porch light on, like she might be expecting them, but most of the parents probably told their kids not to bother her.

A cold wind clattered the branches of the trees and passed between my ribs as well. Kim was scrunched down as close beside me as she could get, her teeth rattling like skeletons' bones.

"I wish they'd hurry," she said, and I did too. Actually, we'd only been there about five minutes, but I was already remembering how warm my house had been. It hadn't been so bad, really, sitting in front of the fire my dad had set in the fireplace, drinking hot cider and answering the door now and then.

Miss Dawson passed in front of her living room window and stopped to look out. Her upper back was so bent that she reminded me of a turtle peering from its shell. I held my breath, though I'm sure she couldn't have seen us anyway. It was strange, squatting there in the dark while she seemed to be looking straight at us. I couldn't breathe properly until she moved away from the window again.

I was just about to ask Kim if she thought the guy taking our order might have figured it for a joke, when a voice came from about two feet behind us. "What're you doing here?" it asked, real quietlike.

Kim's only answer was to topple over onto her nose with a little *"Eeeep!"* She's never been exactly what you could call poised. I practically jumped out of my skin, but I managed to scramble to my feet and turn around.

The boy must have been about our age, but it was obvious his mother hadn't told him he was too old for trick-or-treating. He was wearing the fanciest costume I'd ever seen. I mean, he looked like something out of an old-fashioned book, knickers and high-button shoes and a billed cap. Not a baseball cap, but one of those soft ones with a wide, stubby brim like you see on old men sometimes. He wasn't wearing a mask and he didn't have his face painted or anything like that, but it was all too strange to be anything but a costume.

"What're you doing at my house?" he repeated, more loudly this time. He acted very stern, but I could have sworn he was holding back a laugh.

"Your hou—house?" I stammered. "Nobody lives here except old Miss Dawson. Nobody has lived here but her for just about forever."

The boy didn't answer that. He just stood there, looking us up and down. You would think he'd never seen a couple of girls dressed in sweatshirts and jeans.

Kim had gathered her wits enough to pick herself up off the ground by then.

"What's your name?" she asked, or squeaked, really.

"Prew," the kid said.

"Drew?" I repeated, but the boy shook his head.

"Prew," he corrected.

"Mine's Heather," I told him. "And this is Kim."

He smiled, not a welcoming smile exactly, but like he thought our names were funny. Though I couldn't figure why someone named Prew would think anybody else's name was funny.

"You through trick-or-treating?" I asked.

"Trick-or-treating?" he repeated, like he'd never heard of such a thing. And then before I could decide whether he was joking or just dumb, he asked, "You want to help with a Halloween prank?" He adjusted his cap, pulling it down onto his forehead at a cocky angle, his eyes shining with mischief.

"Uh . . . I guess so. Yeah. Sure," I answered, though I wasn't feeling sure about anything. What else were we about if not a prank, though I wouldn't have thought of using such a funny, old-fashioned word to describe it. Still, whatever this boy had in mind would probably be better than having to explain what we were doing at "his" house . . . or about the pizza truck that was sure to show up any minute. He was probably a visiting relative, a distant grandnephew or something, and if he told Miss Dawson about our pizza "prank," she'd tell our parents for sure.

"What do you want to do?" Kim asked.

"How about hauling a buggy up on top of the school?" Prew came back with.

"A buggy?" Kim and I echoed. Was this strange kid talking about a baby buggy? And where were we supposed to find one of those? I didn't even know anybody who had one.

"Or we could go out to one of the farmer's fields and tip over corn shocks," Prew continued, clapping his hands like he was applauding his own idea. "Or better yet, outhouses right here in town."

*Outhouses!* I had heard of those. They used to sit in people's backyards and they were used for . . . Oh, yuck!

"Last year some of the bigger boys tipped over old Mr. Stanberg's two-holer . . . with him in it! He thought if he sat up in it all night no one would dare try. Was he *upset*!" And he laughed, though whether at the thought of the old man tipped over with the outhouse or at his own pun was hard to tell.

Kim moved in closer to me, and I knew what she was thinking. This kid was a real nut case!

"Of course," Prew added, thoughtfully, "if you're going to tip an outhouse, you do have to be careful not to fall in yourself."

"Ew!" Kim exclaimed, and she turned away, holding her nose.

"Nobody around here—" I started to say, but he wasn't listening.

"I know!" he cried. "I've got a better idea yet!" And he turned and started down the street, motioning us to follow.

I looked at Kim, who looked at me. Then we both shrugged and went after him. I must admit, though, I was hoping this new idea would be an improvement over tipping outhouses. Even nonexistent ones!

"We're going to miss the delivery," Kim hissed in my ear. I shrugged. If you want to know the truth, the whole pizza idea was seeming pretty dumb by this time anyway. And a gust of sharp wind told me it was better to be moving than hanging around in somebody's bare bushes.

So we trotted along after Prew as though it was what we always did on Halloween, follow a boy we'd never met before through the night streets. The leaves crunched underfoot, crisp and dusty, and there was a smell of sweet wood smoke in the air, probably coming from my own house. Only we weren't going toward my house.

"Where are we going?" Kim whispered. She always asks me questions like I'm supposed to know all the answers.

Before I could tell her that I didn't have the faintest idea, Prew stopped in front of the Methodist church. It's the oldest church in town, stone with a square bell tower that holds a real bell. Behind it and to one side, there's a cemetery too. With real ghosts, I suppose. If you believe in such things.

I'd always figured that ghosts appear only to people who believe in them, which left me out for sure. My parents are both scientists, the kind of rational thinkers who answer every question with more facts than anybody wants to hear. When I was a little kid, they even told me the "facts" about Santa Claus, which I thought, even at the time, was a crummy thing to do.

"What are we going to do here?" I asked, not even

trying to keep the sarcasm out of my voice. "Swing a dead cat over our heads to cure warts?"

Kim giggled, her nervous giggle, which isn't much different from her silly one or her downright scared one or her nothing-else-to-do-anyway one unless you know her real well. Prew didn't even glance in our direction. Instead he started along the front walk of the church and turned, abruptly, into the cemetery.

Kim and I followed. "What better place to spend Halloween?" I murmured.

"I don't think the residents give out very good treats, though," Kim answered back. I could tell she was trying to sound totally cool. There was only a small slice of a moon, so as we moved away from the streetlights darkness settled around us like a vampire's cloak.

Kim kept in step with me, practically glued to my side.

Prew stepped up onto the edge of a tombstone near the side of the church and took hold of a low tree limb. "What we're going to do," he explained, as he pulled himself up into the gnarled oak, "is give this town reason to believe in ghosts."

For an instant his white shirt and the white knee stockings below his knickers stood out clearly, bright in the faint moonlight. Then, for just another instant, or perhaps only a fragment of one, I could have sworn the light passed right through him. It was like he was made of glass, or something even less substantial than glass. And then he disappeared behind a screen of dead leaves.

"Let's get out of here!" Kim moaned, but I stayed put.

"He's in the tree," I told her. "And we can go anyplace he can." Then before she could answer, I stepped up onto the edge of the tombstone, too, took hold of the limb, and pulled myself up.

Kim scrambled after me. She's anything but a rational thinker, and I'm sure she wasn't about to be left alone among the gravestones, even a couple dozen steps from the street. It was good she'd followed me anyway, because we hadn't gone farther than the next branch before we saw Prew again, just as substantial as before.

"We're going to toll the bell," he explained as he crawled out onto a thick branch overhanging the roof of the church.

"The way they do when someone dies?" Kim gasped.

"Are you crazy?" I demanded, still following. I'm no dweeb, but it doesn't take a whole lot of brains to figure that if you ring a big, loud church bell when it's not supposed to be ringing, someone will come to investigate. "We'd get caught for sure. Besides, ringing the bell won't make people believe in ghosts. They'd know it was kids."

Prew dropped off onto the flat roof. "We won't get caught because we aren't going to be anywhere near when it's ringing. In fact, no one is, except for our friends here." And he swept a hand in the direction of the dark cemetery. "So folks will just have to blame them. Don't you see?"

I didn't see. I didn't see anything at all, but I decided, reluctantly, that I would give him a chance to show us. Which he proceeded to do.

There were some louvers broken across one window in the bell tower, so Prew climbed through into the musty darkness beyond. We followed. Dozens of pigeons and squirrels had been there before us, and the stone steps were cluttered and slippery. The cemetery below seemed positively friendly in comparison!

Prew moved on ahead to the small room where the monstrous bell hung. Then, groping in the near dark, he located the two bell ropes, each falling through a hole in the platform to a distant floor below. A fat one attached to a big wheel was for pealing the bell and a much thinner one attached to an L-shaped piece of metal was for tolling.

Prew pulled the thin rope up until he had hold of the end, which he then handed to me. "Now we'll take this out and tie it to a branch in the tree, one that moves nicely in the wind." His teeth gleamed when he grinned.

He was right to grin, too, because his idea worked! We tied the rope to a swaying branch, and before we could shinny down the tree and scurry out of the cemetery, the bell had let out three solemn *bongs* and a couple of *tinks*. The tinks were, I suppose, from times when the wind hadn't moved the branch far enough to pull the clapper the whole way. When it really connected, though, it was enough to make the hair on the back of your neck stand up and salute.

By the time we stopped again in the shelter of Miss Dawson's lilacs, I was feeling downright friendly toward this new kid. In fact, I was feeling so friendly, I decided to let him in on the little trick we were playing on his great-aunt. I knew we had missed the fun of seeing her greet the delivery, but still the whole thing was kind of funny to think about.

"Anchovies?" he asked when I had finished explaining about the pizza. "What are they?"

"Fish," Kim told him.

"Little salty, stinky fish," I added. "They make anything they're on taste dreadful."

Prew smiled, a long, slow smile. "A great prank," he said, nodding, but then he glanced toward the house and added, almost sadly, "I guess it's time for me to go in . . . before I'm missed." In the distance, the bell bonged again, an exclamation mark for his words.

"When you get in, why don't you ask Miss Dawson for a piece of anchovy pizza?" Kim giggled.

"Does she know you're out?" I asked, just for something to say. The truth was, I didn't want him to go in. The bell tolled loudly again.

"More or less," Prew said, looking back in the direction of the church. "Anyway, she probably figured it out the first time she heard that." He started toward the house.

I had thought he would go up to the front door, but instead he headed toward the side of the house, where a rickety rose trellis stretched upward toward a second-story window.

Kim called to him in a worried voice, "You're not going to climb that old thing, are you?"

"It's the way I always come out." As Prew spoke, he swung up onto the trellis and began to climb. Kim and I hurried to stand below him, though I don't suppose we would have done him much good if he had fallen. From the church, the bell continued to toll, not quite steadily but in a voice that couldn't be missed. I could hear people, up and down the street, opening their front doors and calling to one another in questioning voices.

The trellis must have been stronger than it looked, because it didn't even tremble as Prew climbed. When he got to the top, he looked down and waved at us. And then he did something amazing. He pulled off his hat and waved with that, letting a mass of dark curls tumble down his back.

"Prew," I found myself saying. "Pru. Prudence." Miss Dawson's name was Prudence. I'd seen it on her mailbox every day of my life, though no one in the town ever used her first name as far as I knew. But what could it mean, this strange girl, named after the old woman, climbing in and out of an upstairs window in her house?

Kim clamped one cold hand on my wrist. "Look! The window! She can't . . ."

I looked. Pru was standing on the very top of the trellis, leaning toward the tightly closed window. There was no way she was going to be able open it from the outside. The wind gusted, the church bell tolled mournfully, and Pru balanced there, high above the ground.

"Be careful," I called. But the bell, sounding again, drowned out my voice.

It was obvious, though, that Pru didn't need any kind of warning from me. She motioned, as if to tell us to watch, and stepped through the closed window. She simply moved through it the way a shadow passes through glass and was swallowed up inside the old house.

Kim and I stood rooted there, side by side, mouths gaping, staring at the blank window. After a moment, we turned to one another, but neither could think of anything to say. Finally, by some unspoken agreement, we started across Miss Dawson's yard, heading for my house. As we passed the front porch, though, the door opened, and the old woman herself appeared on the porch.

"Hello, girls!" she called. "You must have come for a treat. Come in. Come in. I thought no one was going to stop at my house this year."

Kim and I stopped walking as suddenly as if our feet had been caught in a trap. Then, not knowing what else to do, we turned and went toward her.

"You're in luck," Miss Dawson was saying as we climbed the steps to her porch. "Somebody sent me a special Halloween treat."

"A treat?" I managed to stammer.

"Oh," she continued in a confiding way, "it was meant as a prank, I know, but I paid for it so the shop wouldn't suffer. I couldn't possibly eat it all myself, though. I was just hoping some nice youngsters would come by to share it with me."

Down the street, the church bell bonged.

"Someone must have died," Kim said without even a trace of a giggle, but Prudence Dawson only shook her head.

"More Halloween pranks, I think. In fact, I remember a time when I was a little girl . . ."

Her voice trailed off, but she reached up to set an imaginary cap at a jaunty angle, her eyes gleaming with mischief. She held the door wide for us. Just be-hind her on an antique hall table sat an enormous, flat box.

Already I could detect the aroma of anchovies.

# About Marion Dane Bauer

●●●●●●●●

I grew up with my head full of stories. I was born in 1938 in the cement-mill housing at the edge of a small town in Illinois. We were surrounded by the enormous, dusty mill on one side, a corn field on the other, deep woods and the Vermillion River valley on the other.

There were rarely other children for me to play with, so I read, of course. But mostly I made up my own stories. I made up stories as I explored the woods or hiked through the rustling corn stalks. I gathered dolls or marbles or "ladies" made from hollyhock blooms and used them as characters in more stories. And when I happened to have a friend at hand, I told stories, which we both acted out.

Becoming an adult changed only one thing. Now I write my stories down. My first novel, *Shelter from the Wind,* was an American Library Association Notable Book. *Rain of Fire* won the Jane Addams Award. *On My Honor* was a Newbery Honor Book. My most recent books are a novel called *Face to Face* and a nonfiction book, *What's Your Story? A Young Person's Guide to Writing Fiction.*

And I am currently working on some rather gentle ghost stories for younger children and making plans to visit Alaska, where I hope to meet a bear or two . . . for a novel about a girl and a bear. Then there is an idea I have been turning over for more than a year . . . about a fifteen-year-old boy in love with his English teacher. The stories keep coming.

"Triple Anchovies" began with a single question. What if the selves we outgrow were to hang about in some kind of ghostly form? Who can prove they don't? Another story.

Can a Gemini cocker spaniel
find happiness with a Leo owner?

• • • • • • • • • • •

# WHO NEEDS AN
# ARIES APE?

## Walter Dean Myers

**O**kay, so I really love Ol-
lie. I mean, who wouldn't love a six-month-old cocker
spaniel with those big, dark eyes and the most absolutely adorable ears in the whole world? The question,
at least in my mind, is do I love him more because I'm
a Leo and he's a Capricorn? I don't know, but I'll keep
him anyway and I think we'll get along just fine. If
you're wondering what Ollie's being a Capricorn has
to do with anything, I'd have to tell you that it really
started with the Taurean cat that Mr. Jones, the father
of the identicals, sold to Mrs. Davis. On second
thought, maybe I'd better tell you the whole story just
as it happened.

The Jones family moved next door to me in Ellisville
three years ago. I remember them moving in just about

the time I got my second set of braces. Mr. Jones is a tall man, a little on the thin side, and he wears glasses. Nothing special about him particularly. Mrs. Jones is really nice. She always waves hello and she knew my name, which is Ginger, even before I told her. Probably heard it from some of the other kids in the neighborhood. One of the really cool things about the Jones family is that they own a pet shop. My father said it wasn't doing too well, but all the kids still liked it. Another neat thing about the Jones family is that they have two girls my age. And the neat thing about the two girls my age is that they're identical twins.

"You can tell them apart by the way they smile." That's what Billy Moran said. "Denise starts her smile from the left side of her face and Debbie starts her smile from the right side of hers."

That's not true, of course. There was no way that you could tell them apart. The fourteen-year-old identicals, as everyone in the neighborhood calls them, are exactly five feet two inches tall, have brown eyes, and skin that looks as if someone added just a touch of brown to the color of peaches. They both have dimples too.

I like both of them, and they like me. I guess that's why I was the first one that Denise called when their parents were called away to Waterloo. That's where Mrs. Jones was from, and it was her mother who was sick.

"Mom will probably be gone for a couple of days, but Dad'll be back by tomorrow night," Denise said. "We have to feed the animals and make sure all the temperatures are right, stuff like that."

"Are you going to sell pets too?" I asked.

"Dad says we can if a customer comes in and knows what they want," Debbie said. "But he wants us to concentrate on just taking care of the animals while they're gone."

Well, naturally, me being practically the best friend of the identicals, I went over to the store the next morning, which was Saturday. When I got there Debbie had just finished checking the temperature of the water in the fish tanks and made sure that the room temperature was warm enough, and Denise was feeding a positively yucky lizard.

We sat around and talked for a while and listened to some classical music. I wanted to listen to some Michael Jackson tapes, but the identicals said that Michael Jackson's music made the budgies nervous. Then, about four-thirty, in comes Mrs. Davis with a little calico kitten.

Now, I've known Mrs. Davis for about four years. She used to work in the drugstore over on Elm and Third, but now she's retired.

"I really don't think she likes me very much," Mrs. Davis said. "She seems so nervous all the time. I think I should return her before she becomes ill."

"How much did you pay for her?" Debbie (she was wearing a pin with her name on it) asked.

"Oh, that's all right," Mrs. Davis said. "Why don't you just write down that I did return the kitten and I'll settle with your father when he returns."

"Yes, ma'am." Denise was rubbing the kitten gently behind the ears before putting her into a cage.

"Well," said Debbie after Mrs. Davis had left, "did

you see that pin Mrs. Davis was wearing? It was shaped like a big crab. Maybe that's why the kitten didn't like her. She was too crabby. Get it?"

"I got it," I said, "but with any luck I'll get rid of it before it turns into something serious!"

"Where does Dad keep his records, Debbie?" Denise asked.

"They're in the back room in that closet near the window," Debbie said. "But you'd better stay away from them. You remember that Dad wasn't even too keen on letting us open the store while he and Mom were gone."

"I'm not going to do anything stupid," Denise said, making a face at her sister. "I just want to see something, that's all."

When Denise went into the back room Debbie started telling me how whenever they got into trouble it was usually her sister's fault. Then we started talking about the new gym teacher, who was very cute but losing his hair. Debbie said that she thought that men lost their hair because they worried too much. I said the only thing they were worried about was that they were losing their hair. That's what I heard my mom say, anyway.

Then Denise came out from the back room with a big grin on her face like she knew something special.

"So?" I said. "You look like the cat that just swallowed the—"

"That's a no-no in here," said Debbie, putting her hand over my mouth. "But what did you find out, Denise?"

"You remember that crab that Mrs. Davis was wearing?"

"Yes," I said.

"So that means that her sign is Cancer," Denise said. "And the kitten is a Taurus. Obviously, they are not compatible."

"You mind telling me what you're talking about?" Debbie asked.

"And how did crabs get into this conversation?" I asked.

"All of you, I'm sure," said Denise, "have heard of the science of astrology."

"The nonscience," Debbie said. "My science teacher says that astrology is just a superstition, that the stars have no effect on how people get along with each other."

"Did I say that the stars had an effect on how people get along with each other?" Denise had her hands on her hips. "Did I? Did I?"

"No, but you were just about to, I bet," Debbie said.

"What I was going to say," Denise said, holding her nose in the air, "is that astrology only works on animals. That's why Mrs. Davis didn't get along with the kitten. They were born under the wrong stars. She should have had a Libra kitten, and they would have made it just fine."

"I've never heard of that before," I said.

"There are a lot of things that you have never heard of before, Ginger," Denise said. "But that doesn't make them untrue."

That's what Denise was saying, and I had to admit she was right. But then Denise suggested something that sounded pretty good to me. Or at least it did at the time.

"People return pets a lot. Sometimes they say they've made a mistake and they didn't really want the pet, and sometimes they say that there's something wrong with the animal. Dad says the people expect the animals to be like the trained animals you see in television commercials, or they really don't know what to expect," Denise said, "and that's why they bring them back."

"So?" I said, trying to make it sound intelligent.

"So I bet if we did a survey"—Denise was tapping a pencil against the end of her nose—"we'd find out that they were all the wrong signs."

"How do you find out which are the right signs?" I asked.

That's when Denise brought out this book on astrology with all these signs in it, and which ones should work together, and which ones should play sports together, that kind of thing. Then we tried to figure out which ones would be the ones for pets and their owners and Debbie figured out that it was probably the same as the ones telling you which person you should marry.

"You don't marry a goldfish," I said. "You put him in a bowl with an air pump and feed him once a day."

"You bring him home and you take care of him for the rest of his life," Denise said. I noticed that the identicals were both getting excited about the idea. "And if it's a watchdog, he takes care of you for the rest of his life too. Sounds like marriage to me."

Well, it didn't sound much like marriage to me. At

least not any marriage that I had heard about. All the same, I found myself agreeing with the identicals that we should make a survey of all the pets that Mr. Jones had sold over the last six months. That, I want to tell you, was a lot of pets.

What Mr. Jones had was a listing of the exact age of every animal. Sometimes the animal, if it was a pedigreed dog or cat, would have the date of its birth listed on a form. If it wasn't on a form then Mr. Jones would either estimate the time of its birth or get it from the breeders.

"That way he can tell the new owner what to expect," Denise said.

I guess a lot of the people were surprised when either Denise or Debbie called and asked what sign they were. I was surprised that we were doing it, but I was even more surprised when I heard Debbie telling a woman that she would have to bring back a Virgo hamster because it was the wrong sign.

"Did the woman say she was going to bring it back?" I asked.

"This afternoon at three o'clock!" Debbie said, very pleased with herself. She had taken a little white mouse out of its cage and it was clinging to her sweater. "She said she was wondering why it wasn't eating properly."

That's when I looked up me and Ollie. I was born on the twelfth of August, which made me a Leo, and Ollie was born on the third of June, which makes him a Gemini. At first I felt bad, then I decided to fudge it. One of the identicals was on the phone and the other one was looking up the sign of a chimpanzee that Mr.

Jones had sold to the elementary school. He turned out to be an Aries.

"Now, do we go by the principal's birthdate or the teacher who's taking care of him?" Denise asked.

"Who cares whether or not a monkey is an Aries or not?" I said, still thinking about Ollie.

"He's not a monkey," Denise said, "he's an ape!"

"Well, who needs an Aries ape?"

"That is not the question," the other identical said. "The question is whether or not you're going to help us round up the animals who aren't properly matched."

I wouldn't have helped if I were the only one, because I didn't want to get into any trouble. But the identicals called every kid on the block and some in the class that didn't even live near us and that afternoon we were all going around, rounding up animals.

The plan the identicals had for rounding up the animals seemed fine on paper, but it didn't turn out that way. There were animals everywhere. Jimmy Hunter mixed up three guinea pigs so you couldn't tell the Virgo from the two Aries, and Cathy Brown let the iguana she was picking up slip out of the bag when she walked through Memorial Square, and refused to pick it up because she said she was afraid of getting warts.

Of course, not everyone gave up their pets, but a lot of people did. Mostly you could say that dog people and cat people wouldn't give up their animals. On the other hand, fish people, hamster people, some of the parakeet people, and nearly all of the gerbil people gave them up.

Somebody, probably a Pisces person, called the local newspaper and asked what was going on. Everybody showed up at the Joneses' pet shop at the same time. Two kids came with turtles, a man came with a snake wrapped around his neck, two women came with cats just to have their horoscopes read, a reporter came from the local paper, and Mr. and Mrs. Jones arrived in their station wagon.

We found out that Mrs. Jones' mother was okay over in Waterloo, and that Mr. Jones was furious right here in Ellisville. He went around apologizing to all the people who had brought their pets back, and his mouth was smiling, but when he looked at the identicals his eyes weren't smiling, not a bit.

But the funniest thing that happened was that when the story hit the newspaper the next day, people from all over the county started calling Mr. Jones and coming to him to buy pets. It seems that a lot of people believe in astrology. Like I said, it wasn't so much the dog people, or the cat people, but a lot of the others. In fact, Mr. Jones even started putting little tags around the gerbils' necks, which said things like "Hi, I'm an Aquarian" or "Please love me, I'm a Scorpio." I think it's dumb, but now my father said that the Joneses' pet shop is doing very well, so maybe it isn't.

I'm still best friends with the identicals. The other day I took Ollie down to the shop to have his nails trimmed—you have to do that with a cocker spaniel— and Debbie (or maybe it was Denise) said it was sure lucky that Ollie and I were compatible. I said it sure was, but I couldn't help smiling, because according to their charts, we aren't compatible at all. And you know what, I wouldn't swear to this, but I think Ollie smiled too.

# About Walter Dean Myers

• • • • • • • •

Walter Dean Myers is the author of more than twenty books for young readers. *Scorpions* was a Newbery Honor Book winner; and *Motown and Didi: A Love Story, The Young Landlords,* and *Fallen Angels* were all winners of the Coretta Scott King Award. *Mop, Moondance, and the Nagasaki Knights,* a companion to *Me, Mop, and the Moondance Kid* will be published this fall. He lives in Jersey City, New Jersey.

Walter Dean Myers writes:

Reading can open worlds of learning, thought, or pure fun. Writing them does the same thing for me. When I was a child books were my secret friends. I could laugh with them or even cry with them. When I discovered that you could take books home from the library for free, the world became a friendly place for me. I never had to explain to them why I couldn't speak as clearly as the other children, or that I felt bad about not having money for things that other kids seemed to have, or that I wasn't very good at making human friends. Now that I'm grown books are still my friends, but the secret's out.

"The thing about Lavinia was, no matter
how hard she tried not to, she always
ended up seeing things. Dead, that is.
Or dying. Or doomed to die shortly."

• • • • • • • • • • •

# THOSE IN PERIL
# ON THE SEA

## Janet Taylor Lisle

**T**he first time we saw La-
vinia, she looked exactly as if nothing were wrong
with her at all. She had large brown eyes, an upturned
nose, freckles, and she was wearing a pretty red skirt.
A green bandanna held back her hair. She sat at her
desk with her hands folded neatly on top. She was to
be a new girl in our school that year, but there was
something about the way she examined us coming into
the classroom that let us know right away she didn't
feel nervous about it.

We were the nervous ones. Summer vacation was
over. It was the first day of classes. There were all the
usual problems of who'd be in whose room and what
teachers we'd get and which locker and which desk
would be ours for the year.

In the middle of everything, Erica Briggs found out she'd gotten Mrs. Bone for homeroom instead of Miss Alverez like the rest of us, and she made such a terrible screech going away down the hall—"As if she were being slaughtered by an ax-murderer in Central Park," Lavinia would say later—that nice Mr. Picoli, the librarian, who never does anything to anyone, ordered her to the office before classes even started. Everyone gets jumpy on the first day of school.

Lavinia had come to school early, though, and found her locker by herself, and got herself set so that she was in the superior position of being able to say "Hello" to us when we entered the room.

"Hello," we said back.

"There's a dead mouse under the radiator," she said next. That stopped us in our tracks.

"What?! Where?!"

Martha Miller hates mice and rats with a passion, so she put her hand over her eyes and just about fainted on the spot. But Jennifer and I dropped our coats on the floor—we hadn't found our lockers yet—and went to look.

"Right there." Lavinia said.

Jennifer squeaked. *"Eek!"*

It was a dead mouse all right, brownish, lying on its side with its eyes shut tight and its poor little whiskers sticking out from its nose. When we bent over to look closer, we saw that its mouth was open. Inside, the needle-sharp teeth were clenched grimly.

"Oh, ugh," Jennifer said. "I wonder how it died."

Lavinia had not moved from her seat, but she answered anyway.

"Starvation," she said. Her hands stayed folded in front of her. "He got trapped in the school during the summer, and since there was nobody here eating lunch, there were no crumbs, so he starved. Slowly and painfully," Lavinia added, after a pause. "At first I thought it was thirst that got him. But there's a bathroom next door, and mice are smart. Lucky for him he found water there. It's even more horrible to die of thirst."

By now, Jennifer and I had turned around and were staring in amazement at Lavinia, whose name we did not yet even know. If Erica had been with us she would have asked, "Who is this kid, anyway?"

But Erica was at the office, and after she got out of there, she'd be in Mrs. Bone's class for the rest of the year, so Jennifer and I looked at each other for help. Across the room, Martha Miller was still holding her hand over her eyes.

"Get it out!" she was yelling. "I can't stand mice! Get it out of this room!"

At that moment, Miss Alverez came in and we were all called to order. We found our lockers and our desks and finally sat down. After a while, the janitor came, brushed the mouse into a dustpan, and carried it away. The school year began.

"We have a new member of our class," Miss Alverez announced. "This is Lavinia Cosmos. Stand up, Lavinia, and welcome to our school."

"Thank you," Lavinia said, unfolding her hands at last. She stood up and gave us a really wonderful smile.

·  ·  ·  ·  ·

Lavinia was part of our group almost immediately. With Erica gone, a space opened up and Lavinia was the logical choice to fill it. She was nice looking. She was smart in school. She didn't let the teachers boss her around. And she was dependable. When Lavinia said she'd meet you somewhere at a certain time, she was always there. If she borrowed money from you for extra dessert at lunch, she paid you back the next day. She never forgot.

" 'When you borrow from a friend, promptly give it back again,' " Lavinia quoted. "My mother's best friend told me that and I guess I'll always remember it," she said. "Especially now that she's died in that terrible car crash on the New Jersey Turnpike."

"How awful!" Jennifer gasped. "When did it happen?"

"Last year," Lavinia said. "She went through the windshield and was sliced to ribbons when they found her."

"Oh, Lavinia!"

"It's bad on the highways," Lavinia went on. "This morning on the way to school we saw a man who got run over by a truck and beheaded."

"Beheaded!" we all screamed.

"My mother and I tried not to look, but we couldn't help it. We were driving along and suddenly we saw something rolling on the edge of the lane. At first we thought it was a basketball or a soccer ball, but then—"

"Lavinia! Shut up!" we yelled, holding our hands over our ears.

"Sorry," she said. "We did try not to look."

The thing about Lavinia was, no matter how hard she tried not to, she always ended up seeing things. Dead, that is. Or dying. Or doomed to die shortly, like the squirrel she found one day swimming around and around in a clogged storm drain in the school parking lot. We couldn't get to it because a metal grille covered the top to protect the drain from branches and debris. But we could see the poor thing. And we could hear it scrabbling on the side and making desperate little grunts as it grew more and more exhausted and sank gradually lower in the water.

"Lavinia! Why ever did you show us?" We shrieked at her frantically. "What can we do? We can't let it drown!"

"Unfortunately, there's no way we can help," Lavinia replied. Her arms were folded calmly across her chest. "The fire department won't come to rescue a squirrel, and even if they did come, the grille is quite hard to remove. I know because I had a kitten once who fell into a clogged drain like this. By the time they hacked through to her, she was coated with slime and floating facedown in the dirty water."

"Oh, Lavinia!" We wailed. "Don't tell us things like that!"

"The best thing we can do for this squirrel is keep it company in its final minutes," Lavinia informed us. "And maybe sing a song. There's a wonderful old hymn my grandfather taught me before he choked to death last June on a piece of veal chop. It goes like this."

In a clear but terribly sad voice that rang out over

the desperate clawing and panting of the squirrel below, Lavinia began to sing:

> " 'Eternal father, strong to save
> Whose arm doth bind the restless wave
> Who bidd'st the mighty ocean deep
> its own appointed limits keep,
> O, hear us when we cry to Thee
> For those in peril on the sea.' "

It was only when she finished the last line that we
realized how appropriate her grandfather's hymn was,
and burst into tears.

"Oh, the poor animal!" cried Jennifer. "The storm
drain probably does seem like a sea to him. And now
he's in peril on it and no one is strong enough to save
him and . . . oh . . . oh . . . oh!"

She convulsed in sobs and Martha and I put our
arms around her to try to comfort her, and ourselves.
This left only Lavinia to watch over the squirrel. It was
she who let us know, when another minute or two had
passed, that the struggle was over. The squirrel had
sunk.

"He is at peace," she said, while we sniffed and
wiped our noses with our hands.

"But where is he?" Martha quavered, leaning over
and looking down. "I thought you said he'd float."

"He will," Lavinia replied. "In another fifteen to
thirty minutes. We won't see it, though, because the
bell for the end of recess rings in about two minutes."
She checked her watch and then glanced at our snivel-
ing huddle.

"In fact, if we start walking now, we'll probably get

to the school door at exactly the right moment, which will give you time to comb your hair and wash your faces before our next class. You've all gotten into sort of a wrecked condition."

"Okay," we croaked, and followed her across the playground.

Lavinia's grandfather really had died in June, of choking to death on a piece of veal chop that he hadn't chewed properly because his false teeth were loose. Jennifer and Martha and I asked our parents. Not that we didn't believe Lavinia. But there are just so many horrible deaths that can happen around a single person, and we thought Lavinia had had more than her share. The strange thing was, she kept on having it.

Wherever Lavinia was, dogs got run down by cars, cats fell out of trees, people dropped dead at the dentist's or were struck by lightning in the park. Every day, she came to school with fresh tragedies to report, and she described them with such calm, and such immense understanding, that we began to see in her a bravery far beyond our reach.

"I won't be in school tomorrow," she would say, "because my mother and I are going to a very sad funeral. Our mailman was kidnapped at gunpoint a week ago last Thursday, and shot to death and dumped in a wooded lot. Nobody knows why. My aunt Mary says it's the way of the world."

By now, whenever Lavinia mentioned a relative of hers, or a best friend of her parents, we flinched, because the odds were that something dreadful would be

THOSE IN PERIL ON THE SEA

happening to them soon. So it was perfectly natural that Jennifer should finally speak up.

"Please don't tell us what your aunt said, or quote people anymore," she pleaded. "Because then we get to know about them and that makes it so much worse when—"

She did not have to finish her sentence. Lavinia was already nodding and looking sympathetic.

"Of course, I won't," she said to Jennifer. "I'm sorry I didn't think of it before. I certainly don't mean to make anything worse than it is. If I happen to forget again, just remind me, okay?"

Nevertheless, and just as we feared, less than a month passed before Lavinia was telling us she wouldn't be able to go to Martha's birthday party because of her aunt Mary's memorial service in Jersey City.

"Oh, no! What happened?" asked Martha. To be honest, none of us wanted to know, but Martha felt she should inquire, since it was her party.

"Well, it was the strangest thing," Lavinia said. "She fell off the ferry going to see the Statue of Liberty. They've dragged the river for two weeks now, but they can't find the body. That's why—"

She was probably going to say "that's why we're having a memorial service," which is what people have when the body is lost or stolen or not on hand for some reason. Before meeting Lavinia, we never would have known this fact, or even thought about missing bodies. But now we did know, and we knew a lot of other things, too, that we wished we didn't have to, and maybe it was this feeling of being overwhelmed by a whole never-ending, relentless world of dying and deadness that made Jennifer do what she did.

"They've dragged the river for two weeks now, but they can't find the body. That's why—" Lavinia was saying when . . . Jennifer slugged her. She hauled off and socked her right in the nose.

"*Ow!*" screamed Lavinia. She staggered and sat down hard on the tile floor. We were in the girls' bathroom. She cupped her nose with both hands and looked up at us with brimming, furious eyes. Small streams of blood began to ooze through her fingers.

"*Ow-ow-ow-ow!*" she shrieked. Her eyes squeezed shut in pain. A flood of tears gushed down her face.

Jennifer stood looking down at her for a moment, massaging the knuckles of one hand. Then she turned in silence and walked out of the bathroom.

"Jennifer! How could you!" Martha and I screamed together. "Come back! Jennifer! Come back this minute!"

We could see she wasn't about to do that, though. So we bent over Lavinia, who was now a mass of blood, and helped her get to her feet. We brought her wads of paper towels soaked in warm water. We made her hold her head back so the blood would stop pouring out. We tried to wipe off her blouse and skirt, but it was pretty hopeless. Even her socks had blood on them.

Her nose wouldn't stop. In the end we had to take her to the nurse, who put on cold compresses and gave her an aspirin.

"What happened?" the nurse asked.

"She tripped in the bathroom," Martha said.

"And fell against the sink," I added quickly.

Lavinia didn't say anything. She was lying on the infirmary cot holding a giant compress over her mouth and nose. Her eyes were closed. We couldn't tell if she'd heard us or not.

She never spoke to any of us again. She didn't act angry or accuse us of anything. She just stopped being with us, and was careful to keep away from places we were likely to go. From a distance, we saw her checking her watch, arriving on time, smiling at people, borrowing money for dessert. Once, walking down the hall, we heard her telling someone that a bird had gotten into the school library and impaled itself on a desk lamp there. We passed by before we could hear any more.

"Poor Mr. Picoli," Jennifer said.

For a while, we were afraid of Lavinia, especially Jennifer. She stayed out of sight on the playground and had some nightmares about aliens with evil powers trying to zap her when she wasn't looking. But a month went by. Then another month.

"You know, if Lavinia wanted to get us, she'd have done it by now," Martha pointed out, at last. "Even her own aunt took her only two weeks."

This struck us as so hysterically funny, after all the tension we'd been under, that we fell to the ground and rolled around laughing until our stomachs ached. The day was an unnaturally warm one at the end of February. We were on a grassy part of the playground during the long recess following lunch. When we couldn't laugh anymore, we lay on our backs and gazed up at the sky. It was a brilliant blue and curved over us grandly, without a cloud in sight.

"It's like an enormous bowl, isn't it?" I said. "And we live here, underneath, safe and sound in our world."

Beside me, Jennifer slowly shook her head. "It doesn't look like a bowl to me," she said. "It looks like an ocean. It's a deep and perilous sea, and we're floating on the water's surface staring down into it."

Martha gave a little gasp. "But Jennifer, that's terrible! It makes us sound like the poor squirrel that ended up drowning in the storm drain," she said. "It's like in Lavinia's hymn, where people cry for help but no one comes to save them."

Jennifer sat up and looked at us. "That's how it really is, isn't it?" she asked. "If you're alive there's no way you can be saved in the end. You've got to die somehow and nobody can help that."

A sudden horrid chill went through us all. We glanced at each other and looked over our shoulders in fright. We stood up without a word and began to walk toward the school. Faster we walked, faster and faster. Halfway across the playground, we lost our nerve completely and began to run.

By spring, Lavinia was gone. She didn't even finish out the third academic quarter. We heard she was moving to Arizona to be near her father's family. Her father's mother had died suddenly from a heart attack, and now her grandfather needed someone to look after him. Lavinia's parents had both gotten jobs out there.

"They'd bought a house and they were supposed to

start working for the same company. Everything looked great," Martha reported to us one day. She'd been talking to Lavinia's more recent friends.

"What do you mean 'looked great,' " Jennifer asked nervously. "What's this about 'they were supposed to start working'? Did something happen to Lavinia's parents?"

Martha nodded.

"You won't believe it, but I'll tell you anyway," she said.

Then, she told us, while we held our hands over our ears and tried not to listen, how the man who'd hired Lavinia's parents had jumped off a bridge and shot himself in midair, and then his wife, who owned the business, had driven her car off a cliff out of sorrow, so the company was in total grief and chaos and couldn't hire them. But at the memorial service (for nothing was left of either body) a bomb went off and blew up three rows of mourners, and Lavinia's parents were there because they were still hoping to get their jobs back, and were blown to pieces. And they were taken, barely alive, to a hospital where moments after their arrival a weird disease broke out among the doctors, who were choking to death in the halls by the time Lavinia rushed in to find her parents, even though a mad, drug-crazed gunman was on the roof with a sub-machine gun mowing down—

"Stop!" we screamed at Martha. "We don't want to hear this! We don't want to know! Just stop, stop, stop, stop, stop!"

# About Janet Taylor Lisle

· · · · · · · ·

Janet Taylor Lisle worked as a newspaper reporter for ten years before turning to children's fiction. Her first book for children was the original and very funny *The Dancing Cats of Applesap.*

*Sirens and Spies,* her second novel, explores the effect on two sisters of information that they learn about their music teacher when she was a child in France during World War II. Among the honors that *Sirens and Spies* received are citations as an ALA Notable Children's Book, an ALA Best Book for Young Adults, a *Booklist* Editors' Choice, a *School Library Journal* Best Book of the Year, and a Parents Choice Award for children's literature.

*The Great Dimpole Oak* is a fable that was listed as a *Booklist* Editors' Choice, a *Parents Magazine* Best Children's Book of the Year, and a Golden Kite Honor Book from the Society of Children's Book Writers.

*Booklist* noted that "Lisle examines the nature of reality and the hint of magic that pervades the everyday world" in describing *Afternoon of the Elves,* which was a 1990 Newbery Honor Book.

Lisle's most recent novel is *The Lampfish of Twill.*

Janet Taylor Lisle grew up in Connecticut. She holds a B.A. degree in English from Smith College and studied journalism at Georgia State University. She now lives in New Jersey with her husband and their daughter, Elizabeth.

Not everyone would agree that
Timmy is the best dog in the world,
but he certainly has his moments.

• • • • • • • • • •

# THE BEST DOG
# IN THE WORLD

## Carol Snyder

**I** have this dog, Timmy,
who I absolutely love. All right, so he does turn into a
snarling beast whenever the mailman comes closer
than a block away. Okay, so he does snap at anyone
that comes near his food or touches his collar or moves
his foot too fast if it's resting nearby. My friends don't
understand that Timmy just has some rules. Okay, lots
of rules. But he's still the best dog in the world. I don't
see why they're afraid to come to a sleepover at my
house.

I admit, Timmy does look part wolf and has these
crazy hairs growing out of his ears and a tail like a
question mark. And yes, it is also true that he ate my
entire box of sixty-four colors of Crayola crayons
(even raw umber, which is disgusting), several quar-

ters, nickels, and dimes, and two electric blankets. But he was just upset because I'd gone to my friend Elayne's for a slumber party.

Now, Elayne has this little poodle, Kupee, who everyone loves. He greets each friend with licks and tail wags and cuddles up under your chin so warm and snuggly. He even let each of us brush his curly fur and put bows and barrettes in his head.

Now, Timmy is just not the cuddly type, that's all. And the idea of anyone putting a bow or a barrette anywhere near Timmy's head makes me double over laughing.

So tonight should be pretty interesting. Elayne, Sheila, and Marsha, my three best friends, are, as they put it, "risking life and limb" to sleep over at my house. I told them I would have a heart-to-heart talk with Timmy, and not to worry.

"Yeah, a talk," Sheila said, sarcastically. "That'll do the trick. Your dog doesn't even listen when your father says 'get down,' and he's a zillion times Timmy's size."

"Sure," Elayne said. "I'm not about to relax as long as Timmy has a single pointed tooth in his mouth."

"Maybe you'll get through to him like lion tamers at the circus." Marsha always believes in me.

All right, so I have a dog with an attitude. But he always listens to me. When I have a problem, I can tell him everything. I can cry into his wiry fur. I can tell him good exciting news and he jumps up and puts his paws on my shoulder and licks me on the nose with happiness. If I'm home alone with him while my parents are at work, and I hear a scary noise, all I have to say is, "What was that, Timmy?" and he charges through the house barking and snarling and I'm not afraid anymore. He's the best dog in the world. You just have to get to know him, that's all. With this slumber party maybe my friends will see how sweet and wonderful he can be.

"C'mere, Timmy," I say, and he comes over and puts his chin in my lap. I lean over and kiss his one soft spot —on his snout—and move away really quick because he sometimes lifts his head up suddenly and pops you in the nose—by accident, of course. "I have to talk to you heart-to-heart." He looks right up at me with his serious brown Bambi eyes and I love him more than ever. He sidles up closer and puts his head in my hand to be petted.

"Now, you know I understand that you're hyper and have rules. But you have to be very gentle and good tonight and not bite anyone or even snarl, so Sheila, Elayne, and Marsha don't get scared when they sleep here. Okay?" He perks his ears up. "Can I count on you?" He wags his tail and turns his head to one side.

He barks once. I think that means "yes" and when he barks twice it means "no." My father says that a dog with a brain the size of a pea can't figure that out, but if I want to believe it, go ahead.

Then I accidentally touch his collar and he shows his teeth to me, the pointy ones. Elayne, Sheila, and Marsha will be arriving any minute. I've got two bags of potato chips, microwaveable popcorn, and lots of orange soda. Everything's under control but Timmy. I hope that an hour from now Elayne, Sheila, and Marsha have not raced out of here screaming and gone home.

The doorbell rings. Timmy races to the door, barking furiously. I let my friends in. They've got sleeping bags and overnight cases and Timmy is trying to sniff everything and everyone at once. He zeroes in on Elayne's things and starts to paw at them and sniff some more.

"Get him away," Elayne says.

"He probably smells your dog, Kupee," I explain. Timmy's really a very nice dog. The best dog in the world, to be exact.

Elayne gives me a look like I'm crazy and starts to drag her sleeping bag to get it away, but Timmy attaches himself to the end of it and drags along. Timmy arches his back. The more Elayne pulls forward, the more Timmy pulls back, making this growling noise.

"He thinks you're playing tug-of-war with him," I say.

"Well, explain to him that I'm not playing tug-of-war and he better cut it out before he rips my sleeping bag with his dumb, sharp, pointed teeth."

"Timmy, be good!" I command and pull the bag out of his mouth, pulling my finger away barely in the nick of time.

"Yuk!" Elayne says. "He slobbered all over my sleeping bag. I'm not sleeping on this!"

In the meantime, Sheila is huddled in a corner waving her hand and saying, "Back! Back!" Timmy keeps bringing her this pink Spalding ball and dropping it at her feet.

"He's being friendly," I explain. "He's sharing his favorite toy. Just throw it and he'll run and chase it.

Really. There's nothing to worry about. He's a very sweet dog. The sweetest dog in the world."

"You want me to touch that disgusting ball he's drooled all over?" Sheila asks.

"He just wants to chase something. It's his favorite game," I explain. How was I to know she would kick the ball across the room?

One very basic rule Timmy has is: *No unexpected movement of feet is allowed.* So, of course, he tries to bite her shoes and she screams and that scares him. This is going to be some slumber party!

"Why don't you lock him in one of the rooms?" Marsha suggests, reasonably.

"I can't lock him in my parents' bedroom because he'll be angry and when he gets angry he tears things up by grabbing them in his teeth and shaking his head from side to side, holding one end down with his paws, his rear end up in the air. Their matching bedspread and drapes will have matching teethmarks."

"I get the picture," Sheila says. "So lock him in the bathroom. Just take the towels out."

"Yeah," says Elayne and Marsha.

"It's a good idea," I say, "except we'd have to get him into the bathroom first and he has this attitude about the bathroom because he hates to get a bath."

Now Sheila starts to giggle. "I think the person who gives Timmy a bath must be the bravest person in the world," she says.

"Oh, it's not so bad. I just wear a bathing suit and gloves."

"Notify *Teen Magazine* fashion page of that sight," Elayne says, and we all laugh.

Usually around this time at a slumber party we're all sitting around on the bed bored, trying to figure out what to do all night. You have to stay up all night at a slumber party. Everyone knows that, or at least until a parent yells out, "Girls! Enough is enough!" But my parents will be out very late at a wedding. I'm too old for a baby-sitter and rather than leave me alone, three trustworthy friends and Timmy puts my parents' minds at ease.

Well, tonight we wouldn't have to figure out what to do. It will probably take all night to get Timmy locked in the bathroom. Then an idea comes to me. "Popcorn!" I say.

"Did I miss something?" Marsha asks, confused. "How did we get from Timmy to popcorn?"

"Timmy loves popcorn. We love popcorn. Let's nuke some and leave a trail of it leading into the bathroom."

"You're on," Sheila says. "I'll just sit up on your countertop till he's locked up. Okay?"

"Okay," I say. The girls make a dash for the kitchen and get up onto the countertop sitting cross-legged, with Timmy slipping and sliding on the tile floor trying to catch them because they've made a sudden move, which is definitely breaking a rule.

I put the bag of corn in the microwave, direction-side up, and soon we hear the popping start. So does Timmy. I'd forgotten how excited he gets when he thinks he's going to have popcorn. So now Timmy starts leaping in the air and the girls are all screaming again and I'm screaming, "Down, Timmy. Get down, you sweetie ole dog."

I quickly leave a trail of popcorn into the bathroom

and race out of it and close the door just as Timmy gets to the last kernel of corn.

"Sorry, Timmy," I say. "I have to do this. I'll make it up to you tomorrow. I promise. I'll get you those special doggy treats you love. I'll scratch you behind your ears the way you like best, and I'll take you for a long walk to the park where the good doggie smells are."

Now Timmy's scratching at the door and barking, but my friends are happy. We have popcorn and soda and curl up on the bed and have potato chips and soda. And then just orange soda and more orange soda because we're so thirsty from the chips. We talk about all the boys in our class, and which teacher is the grossest, and whether we should have our hair cut short or let it grow so long we can sit on it. And then we have some more soda. And then we realize all at once that we all have to go to the bathroom very badly, and we all know who is in the bathroom. The best dog in the world.

I open the bathroom door and Timmy comes flying out like a bucking bronco from its stall at a rodeo—a dog gone wild from being locked up. Jumping and licking everyone. Sheila and Marsha and Elayne are shrieking and giggling at the same time—sort of like hysterics.

"He's just happy to be free," I try to explain. "You can't fault him on that."

I guess they agree or else it's just because they have to go to the bathroom so badly, but everyone calms down. We all lock ourselves in the bathroom and try out make-up and do each other's hair and polish our toenails and wiggle them dry. When we open the door

# FUNNY YOU SHOULD ASK

Timmy practically falls in. He sneezes and sneezes from the nail-polish smell and we dash into the family room.

As we open up the sofabed I say, "Now, just let me explain a few of Timmy's rules: One: *Don't touch his collar.* Two: *Don't move your feet suddenly, especially when he sleeps with us on the sofabed.*"

"Sleeps with us on the bed?" Sheila screams and pretends to faint.

"You gotta be kidding," Elayne says.

"You are kidding, aren't you?" Even Marsha speaks out.

"But he always sleeps with me. Right next to me, under the blanket, his head on my pillow. Ever since he was a new little puppy. Just don't move your feet and he won't bother you, except sometimes he'll twitch his legs when he's dreaming about running or chasing the mailman or something."

The bed is made up. We climb in and put the TV on with the remote to watch the late-night movie. Timmy jumps in and we all stay perfectly still and everyone is okay until Elayne's mosquito bite on her leg starts to itch and she tries to scratch it with her toe.

Timmy's fur bristles up like a porcupine and he arches his back like a hissing cat and he tries to bite the moving blanket. Suddenly the bed is empty. My friends are gone into various closets or behind drapes.

"Timmy, be good!" I command. "You're spoiling my party!" I guess I really sound angry because he lowers his head and looks up at me just with the whites of his eyes, looking all guilty and pitiful and I just feel all sorry for him. I don't think anything can save this slumber party. Even very best friends have a limit, and I won't blame them if they call their parents to be picked up and taken home to their nice, peaceful, safe rooms for a good night's sleep.

But then the late-night movie is interrupted with a bulletin about a riot at the prison downtown and how three dangerous fugitives are on the loose and everyone should make sure their doors and windows are locked and not let anyone in.

Suddenly there are three leaps and landings and Sheila, Elayne, and Marsha are huddled with me in the sofabed. And we all look at each other scary-eyed and then there's a fourth leap and Timmy stands at the foot of the bed staring at us. And at the same moment we all pat the pillows beside us and Elayne even says it out loud.

"Here, Timmy, Timmy, sweetie ole dog. You can sleep next to me tonight."

So here we are. All together. My slumber party a success, my friends all agreeing that the best dog in the world will keep us safe . . . even from fugitives.

"Good night, Elayne," Marsha says.

"Good night, Sheila," Elayne says.

"Good night, Marsha," Sheila says.

"Good night, sweetie ole dog, best dog in the world," I say.

*"Grrrrrrrrr!"* Timmy growls, and we all get very, very still.

# About Carol Snyder

• • • • • • • •

I can pinpoint the exact day I decided to become a writer, because I wrote it down. I was in seventh grade in Brooklyn, New York, and faithfully wrote in a red leather diary each day. Spelling definitely did not count. On March 31, 1954, appears this entry:

> When I grow up I want to be a (gernalist).
> I went to the library and got a (pamflet)
> on (Gernalism) for Boyscouts.

It took five years of apprenticeship and publishers' rejections to have my first book, *Ike and Mama and the Once-a-Year Suit*, published in 1978. I jumped for joy. My husband and two daughters jumped with me. I wrote four more books in the series about an immigrant family and the cooperative multicultural neighborhood in which they live in the South Bronx of the 1920's: *Ike and Mama and the Block Wedding* (AJL Book Award, 1980), *Ike and Mama and the Once-in-a-Lifetime Movie, Ike and Mama and Trouble at School,* and *Ike and Mama and the Seven Surprises* (AJL Book Award, 1986).

I went on to write *The Great Condominium Rebellion,* about the troubles of Stacy and Mark, preteenagers when they visit their grandparents at a seniors' retirement community in Florida. As my own daughters experienced their teen years I wrote about today's kids and family relationships in *Memo: To Myself When I Have a Teenage Kid,* a Children's Choice Book and *The New York Times* recommended book.

*The Leftover Kid* is a humorous story about a latchkey kid, the only kid left at home, who enjoys having the house to herself until an invasion of older brothers and sisters and grandparents and baby nephew all return to the nest.

New York City is the setting for my next book, *Leave Me Alone, Ma,* which seems to be how every conversation creative fourteen-year-old Jaime Newman has with her mother ends up (an IRA/CBC Children's Choice Award Winner and American Bookseller Pick of the List, 1987). *Dear Mom and Dad, Don't Worry,* (The New York Library Books for The Teenage 1991 Selection) about thirteen-year-old Carly's accident and her sometimes painful, sometimes humorous road to recovery followed. With our children grown, my husband and I are enjoying the return to our roots, having moved to New York City after living in Bridgewater, New Jersey, for over twenty-three years.

Besides lecturing, I'm working on a new young teen novel as well as several picture books that will be published next year. *The Good Night Game* will be fun for all you baby-sitters out there.

I had a wonderful time writing "The Best Dog in the World," when I was asked to submit a short story for this anthology. It was inspired by a conversation.

"Remember your dog, Timmy?" a childhood friend had said to me last summer.

"Of course I remember Timmy," I answered. "He was the best dog in the world."

"Are we talking about the same dog? Timmy was the

worst dog. He looked like a wolf and he tried to bite anyone who moved a toe," my friend insisted.

"You just didn't understand him," I said.

After that, I sought out relatives and longtime friends to ask their best memories of Timmy. Answers ranged from "Best? There was no best" to "The one time he didn't bite me."

So I wrote this story to explain about Timmy, to give him a place in literature, because he was my dog and my friend from when I was nine years old until long after he's been gone. Because to me he'll always be *the best dog in the world!*

Miri and her new friend have a lot
to learn about each other—like why
there's a dead fish on Miri's table
and why Jenny's mother washed a pig.

• • • • • • • • • • •

# MIRI'S NEW FRIEND

## Miriam Chaikin

**M**iri lived in Plainfield.
Her father taught English literature in the college in
town. Her mother worked as part-time librarian, and
took yoga classes to relax. Miri went to the Kennedy
School, in Plainfield. Sunday mornings, though, she
went to the Hebrew school at the Jewish Center.
There, she learned to read and write Hebrew, and
about the Bible.

It was Sunday. Miri came home from Hebrew
school. Her mother was busy in the kitchen.

"There's a new teacher at Papa's college," her
mother said. "They moved in around the corner. Papa
went to get them. They're coming for brunch."

"Do they have children?" Miri asked.

"A little girl—Julie."

"How old is she?" Miri asked.

"About your age."

Yossi, Miri's little brother, came into the kitchen carrying a basin. He took it with him wherever he went. He liked to sit in it.

"Did you tell the teacher about me?" he said to Miri. He said the same thing every day. Every day, she gave the same answer.

"They're saving a seat for you, for when you're old enough."

"Wash your face," Miri's mother said. "They'll be here soon."

Miri went into her room. She looked in the mirror. Her face was clean enough. But her hair was messy, and she picked up the comb.

"And comb your hair," her mother called.

"I am combing my hair," Miri called back.

"And put on your new shoes!"

Miri stopped combing her hair. She was *not* going to put on her new shoes. "I don't want to—"

"Why not?" her mother called.

"I want the bottoms to stay clean."

"That's the most ridiculous thing I ever heard," her mother called.

"If the bottoms get dirty, they won't be new anymore," Miri said.

She took the shoe box from the closet, opened it, looked at the shoes, then put back the box.

"Wear something nice," her mother called.

Miri put on a different T-shirt. But she kept on her same shorts and sneakers, and went into the living room.

Yossi was in there, sitting in his basin. He had filled it with strips of old newspaper and sat shoving the pieces around. He liked the sound it made. Miri wondered why he looked different.

"You look funny," she said.

"I'm an airplane," he said, sticking out his arms and making a buzzing sound with his lips.

"It's not that," she said. Then she realized what it was. His hair had been combed. His curls were gone. He didn't look like himself with his hair all neat like that.

Outside, in the driveway, there was the sound of tires on gravel.

"They're here!" Miri's mother said, going to the door.

Miri's father came in with the new people. Miri stared at the girl. She was wearing a party dress! For brunch! *Yick!* Miri thought.

"Miri, this is Julie," Miri's mother said, pushing Miri on top of the girl.

Miri stepped back. She didn't feel like it, but she told herself to be polite. Her parents would have plenty to say later, if she wasn't. "You want to see my room?" she said to Julie.

"Okay," Julie said, following Miri. She noticed Yossi. "What's he doing in a pot?" Julie asked, stopping to stare.

"He likes to sit in it," Miri said.

"Have you got a dog?" Yossi asked Julie.

"No," Julie said.

"I want a dog," Yossi said.

"We have a bird," Julie said. "A parakeet."

"A bird? Phooey!" Yossi said.

"What's wrong with a bird?" Julie asked.

"You can't kiss a bird," Yossi said.

"Yes . . . you . . . can . . ." Julie said, not sounding too sure.

"Come on," Miri said, hurrying the girl along.

In her room, she showed Julie her toys and school books.

"My mother says you study Hebrew," Julie said. "What does it look like?"

Miri knew that Julie's family was Christian. She showed Julie the Hebrew book, and let her look at the writing. Then she showed her the box with her new shoes, and other things.

"Come and eat!" Miri's mother called.

Miri and Julie came to the kitchen. Everyone was seated around the table. Yossi's basin was on a chair and he was in the basin. On the table were all the things Miri's family liked to eat for brunch on Sunday.

Julie sat down and jumped up again. *"Eee"* she shrieked, backing away.

"What is it?" her mother asked.

"There's a dead fish on the table," Julie said.

Julie's parents laughed. "It's smoked fish," Julie's mother said.

"It's delicious," Julie's father said.

Julie covered her eyes. "It's looking at me," she said.

Miri thought everyone, even Christians, ate smoked fish for Sunday brunch.

Miri's mother got up and put the fish on top of the refrigerator, in back. "There's plenty to eat without it," she said. She glanced over the table and called out the items: "Bagels, rolls, cheeses, smoked salmon slices, black and green olives, jams, and avocado salad . . ."

"And it all looks scrumptious," Julie's mother said, and took salmon from the serving plate and a bagel from the bread basket.

Everyone ate. Miri noticed that Julie mostly stared up at the fish, on top of the refrigerator. When brunch was over, the company left. Miri's mother took down the fish, wrapped it in wax paper and put it inside the refrigerator. "We'll have it later," she said, and began to clear the table.

"Ma, did you hear what she said about the fish?" Miri asked.

"A smoked fish does look kind of strange, if you've never seen one before."

"And did you see that stupid dress she was wearing?" Miri said.

Miri's mother looked at Miri's feet. "What about your stupid sneakers!" she said. "I thought you were going to wear the new shoes."

"I didn't say so," Miri said.

"What are you saving them for? Soon, your feet will be too big. They're rotting in the box."

"They're not rotting," Miri said. "You should see how nice they look."

Her mother stared down at her. "Well, young lady, you are definitely wearing the new shoes to Jenny's party. Julie's invited too. She doesn't know anyone. Be nice to her."

Miri made a face. She had forgotten about Jenny's party. She did not care for parties. Mostly because she did not like to dress up. And she was not crazy about seeing Julie again.

Later, she put on a dress, and went into the living room to show herself to her mother. "How do I look?" she said.

Her mother put down the newspaper she was reading. She looked Miri over, starting at the top. "V-e-r-y pretty," she said. When she got to Miri's feet, she stood up. "Go put those shoes on this very minute," she said.

Miri went to her room and put on the shoes. Luckily, the floors were all carpeted. The soles of her new shoes would stay clean in the house. She took some tissue paper and returned to the living room. There was a piece of uncarpeted floor at the edge of the living room, and she jumped over it and onto the rug.

"What was that for?" her mother said.

"I don't want to get the bottoms dirty."

"How are you planning to get to Jenny's house, fly?" her mother said. She shook her head, then shook the paper. "Honestly . . ." she said.

Miri's father and Yossi came home. They had been out. "What's that on your feet?" Yossi asked Miri.

"Shoes. What does it look like?" Miri said.

"Helmets," Yossi said.

Miri's father looked at the shoes. "They're pretty," he said.

Miri's mother got up. She took off her glasses. "If I hear one more word about the shoes . . ." she said.

It got very quiet. Everyone knew when Miri's mother meant business.

"Let's go," Miri's father said to Miri's mother. Miri

knew her father was driving her mother to a yoga class.

"Grandma'll be here any minute," Miri's mother said from the door. "When she comes, you can go." Miri's father was starting the car. Miri's mother closed the door.

"Don't forget Jenny's present!" she called through the door.

Outside, one car pulled away and another arrived. A moment later, Grandma entered. "Hello, my darlings," she said, kissing first Yossi, then Miri. "Oh, what beautiful shoes," Grandma said to Miri.

Miri was glad her mother wasn't around to hear the word. She took the present. And she perched herself on the heels of her shoes and went to the door.

Yossi was sitting in his basin. Grandma was sitting on the floor, next to him, and shredding paper into the basin for him.

"Grandma?" he said.

"Yes, dear?"

"Do birds pooh?" Yossi said.

"See you later," Miri said, and left.

She couldn't walk on her heels. It was too hard. So she walked a few steps, wiped the soles of her shoes with the tissue, walked a few steps. Soon, she was at Jenny's house, giving Jenny her present.

Miri noticed Julie on the other side of the room. She would never have believed it. But Julie was even more dressed up this time. Plus she was wearing shiny black shoes with a little button at the side, and carrying a purse with purple ribbons that hung down. "Yick!" Miri said and turned away. But Julie saw her and came running.

"Hi, Miri," Julie said.

"Hi, Julie," Miri answered.

"The party's in the backyard," Jenny's mother said. "Jenny, take the children outside."

Miri and the other children followed Betsy into the kitchen. The floor had no carpet. Miri stopped at the sink, wet her tissue, and wiped the soles of her shoes.

"What did you do that for?" Jenny asked.

"To clean my shoes," Miri said.

"The bottoms?" Jenny asked.

Miri pretended not to hear. As she followed Jenny to the back door, she saw a huge piece of meat sitting out in the open on the counter, like a roasted turkey. But it was no turkey. "What's that?" Miri asked.

"Ham," Jenny said.

*"Eeuuu!"* Miri said, making a face.

"What's wrong?" Jenny's mother asked.

"Ham is pig," Miri said. "A pig is dirty. We're not allowed to eat it."

"It is *not* dirty," Jenny said. "My mother washes everything first."

"You eat dead fish in your house," Julie said.

Miri despised Julie. "It wasn't dead!"

"Was it alive?" Julie asked.

Jenny's mother said to Miri, "Well, we *are* allowed to eat ham. And we love it. It's not for your party, anyhow. Other company is coming later."

Jenny opened the back door and everyone went outside.

Miri was glad to see that the party table was on the

cement part of the yard, and not on the grass and dirt. Miri hurried to sit beside Michael, a boy in her class. She hoped Julie would find someplace else to sit. But Julie ran over and plunked herself down on the other side of Miri.

There were lots of goodies on the table—chips, pretzels, little heart candies with messages like *I love you,* other candies, and lots to drink. Miri took some chips and heart candies and put them on the paper plate in front of her. Then Jenny came around and gave each one a favor.

Miri was disappointed in hers: a Hi-Li board and ball. She looked at Julie's: a cute little doll. Julie seemed just as disappointed as she was.

"I hate what I got," Miri said.

"Me too," Julie said.

"I like what you got," Miri said, eyeing the doll.

"I like what you got," Julie said. "Let's change."

They did.

The cake was cut and Jenny blew out the candles and everyone got a piece of cake and sang "Happy Birthday." Then Jenny's mother said the party was over.

The children went back into the house, to leave from the front door. In the kitchen, Miri stopped at the sink to wet a fresh piece of tissue and wiped the bottoms of her shoes.

"Are you doing that again?" Jenny asked. Miri didn't answer. She saw Jenny make a crazy sign over her ear. The other children laughed, but Julie did not. She was the only one who didn't. Miri wet the tissue once more, for the walk home, said, "Thank you," to Jenny's mother, and went out.

She and Julie walked home together. Julie played the Hi-Li as she went. Miri was surprised to see how good Julie was at it. She hit the ball every time. Miri named her doll "Partyface." When she stopped to wipe her shoes, the paper fell apart in her hand.

"Awwww!" she said. "Now my shoes will get dirty. They won't be new anymore."

Julie opened her purse and gave Miri a hanky. "Use this," she said.

Miri stared. A hanky! A hanky? "It'll get dirty," she said.

"That's okay," Julie said, hitting the ball, catching it on its way back, hitting it again.

When they reached Miri's house, Miri went in and Julie walked on home.

"Is that you, Miri?" Miri's mother called from the kitchen.

Miri went into the kitchen. Her mother was slicing onions. "Did you have a nice time?" her mother asked through teary eyes.

"I got this doll," Miri said.

"Sweet," her mother said, squinting her tears away.

"Where's Yossi?" Miri asked, looking about.

"Papa took him to the pet shop."

"Is he getting a dog?"

"No," Miri's mother said. "He wanted to see the birds—for some reason."

Miri went to her room and changed into her shorts, T-shirt, and sneakers. She inspected the bottoms of her shoes before putting them away. They were darker than before, but still pretty clean. She put Partyface on her pillow, took Julie's hanky, and went into the kitchen.

"Ma," she said. "Look at this. Julie gave it to me, to wipe my shoes."

"Put it in the laundry," her mother said, pouring oil in a pan on the stove and lighting a flame under the pan.

"A hanky, Ma!" Miri said. "She let me clean my shoes with her hanky!"

"Put it in the laundry," her mother repeated, and threw the onion slices into the pan.

Miri put the hanky in the laundry.

"Ma," Miri said. "Jenny's mother cooked a pig. But it was clean, she washed it first."

Miri's mother shook the pan. "She what?" she said, squinting and squooshing up her nose.

"Cooked a pig. But it was clean, she washed it first," Miri repeated.

"Onions make so much noise—I can't hear anything," her mother said, giving the pan another shake.

Miri went to the side of the counter where the phone was. "Ma, do you have Julie's mother's number?" she asked.

"Under B—Barth," Miri's mother said. "It's the last number. Don't talk long, I'm expecting a call," she added.

"I won't," Miri said. She found the number and dialed.

Julie's mother answered.

"Can I talk to Julie?" Miri said.

Julie got on the phone.

"Hi, Julie, it's me, Miri," Miri said. "Can you come over?"

Julie didn't answer right away. Miri thought it was because of the fish. "Don't worry about the fish," she said. "It's gone."

"I went to ask my mother," Julie said into the phone. "She said okay."

Miri hung up. "Where is the fish?" she asked her mother.

"In the refrigerator," her mother said.

"Please eat it right now. Julie's coming over. I don't want her to see it and get upset again."

Her mother gave the pan a shake, moved it to a back burner, and shut off the gas. She stared at Miri.

"I will eat the fish when I'm good and ready, and not a moment before! Is that clear?" she said.

Miri turned away. There was no point in talking to her mother when she was like that. Soon her mother would go into her room and do deep breathing to relax. She learned it in her yoga class. After that, she would be all right again.

Miri went to the door to wait for Julie.

# About Miriam Chaikin

• • • • • • • •

Miriam Chaikin is the author of more than twenty books for children.

She was an editor-in-chief of books for children before she began writing full-time. Her first book, *I Should Worry, I Should Care,* tells of Molly, a little Jewish girl growing up in Brooklyn at the start of World War II. Four more "Molly" books followed.

She has written several books about Yossi, a Hasidic Jewish boy, including *Yossi Asks the Angels for Help.* Another series of books that she wrote describes Jewish holidays. Her adaptation of *Exodus,* illustrated by Charles Mikolaycak, won the National Jewish Book Award for an illustrated book, and *A Nightmare in History: The Holocaust 1933–1945* was named an ALA Notable Book for Children. Miriam Chaikin won the Sydney Taylor "Body-of-Work" Award in 1985, which is presented by the Association of Jewish Libraries.

Miriam Chaikin lives in New York City and spends a few months of each year in Israel.

•••••••••••••••

# CLASSROOMS AND CORRIDORS

Going to the school dance should be fun.
It's *not* supposed to be dangerous.

• • • • • • • • • •

# BREAK A LEG

## Joel Schwartz

**I** wouldn't have gone to the "Getting to Know You" dance at school if it hadn't been for my father. He wouldn't have talked to me about it if it hadn't been for my mother. She wouldn't have talked to him about it if it hadn't been for my best friend Myron's mother. My best friend's mother wouldn't have talked to my mother about it if it hadn't been for my best friend. Myron wouldn't have talked to his mother about it if I hadn't talked to him about it, so I guess I'm to blame for everything.

It's not that I don't like dances and it's certainly not that I don't like girls. It's just that, well, all the twelve-year-old girls in the world are much taller than all the twelve-year-old boys. I wouldn't mind having to look at them straight in the eye, but having to look up all the time is embarrassing and it hurts my neck too. When you dance with a girl, they are supposed to be able to put their head on your shoulder, not their chin on your head.

So when Myron asked me at lunch, "Are you going to the 'Getting to Know You' dance?"

I said, "Are you kidding? Nobody's going to that dance."

Myron took a giant bite of his sandwich and said, "Emrymoday ish gowig."

"Every Monday, what did you say?" I asked.

Myron wiped a large glob of mustard off his chin with his sleeve. "I said, everybody I know is going." Myron looked at the glob of mustard that now decorated his sleeve and without hesitation ground it into his pants. "Everybody, that is, except you."

I stared down at the spot on Myron's pants and then up at a new glob on his chin. At this rate, by the end of lunch, he would be wearing palomino-colored pants and a white shirt with gold cuffs. "Name one person who's going."

"Me!"

"Besides you."

"Todd Murray."

"Mr. Murray, our math teacher?" Myron nodded. "He has to go. He's the chaperon. Besides, teachers don't count."

"Come on, go." I shook my head no. "For me?" I shook my head no again. "Why not?" This time the mustard had migrated up both cheeks.

"Why do you use so much mustard on your sandwich?" I asked, purposely changing the subject.

"Because I hate the taste of the meat," replied Myron.

"If you hate the taste of the meat so much, why don't you put a different kind of meat on your sandwich?"

"If I put on the meat that I liked, I wouldn't put on any mustard, and I like mustard on my sandwich." I stood up to go. "Not so fast. Why won't you go to the dance? Are you too chicken to go?"

"I don't want to talk about it anymore," I replied. "Finish eating your mustard sandwich and have a good time at the dance. You can tell me about it on Monday."

I thought I had heard the last of it, but after dinner that night my father asked me to go into the den because he wanted to talk to me about something. This usually means I've done something wrong and my mother has delegated my father to handle it.

"I've cleaned up my room," I said. "I did all my homework. I'll read a book for half an hour before I go to sleep, and I took out the trash."

My father smiled. "Why aren't you going to the 'Getting to Know You' dance?"

"How do you know that?" I asked.

"Your mother was talking to Myron's mother and—"

"I don't want to go, that's all. What's the big deal?"

My father lit his pipe and leaned back in his chair. This usually meant he was going to tell me a story about himself when he was my age. "When I was your age and just starting seventh grade like you, my school had a 'Getting to Know You' dance too, and I didn't want to go either. My dad sat me down, just like this, and said to me, 'I'll bet you're a little afraid to go to the dance.' 'Afraid?' I replied. 'I'm not afraid of any school dance.' 'Not of the dance,' he continued, 'but of the girls. Girls can be scary at your age. They act like they feel more comfortable in social situations than boys, but they're just as scared as you are. Go to the dance, act like you know what you're doing, and I'll bet you'll have a good time.' I didn't want to admit it then, but what your grandfather said to me that day made sense and I decided to go to the dance. The night of the dance my father drove me to the school and as I got out of the car he said 'Break a leg.' That's an expression actors use when they want to wish another actor good luck on the night of a performance. I think he did that purposely because he knew I'd have to be a good actor that night to hide my nervousness. I was nervous that night, but I covered it well and I ended up having a great time. Think about it."

I sat by myself in the den for a long time after Dad left and thought about what he just said. Usually what Dad says is either dumb or old-fashioned. This time he surprised me with something right on. Was he getting smarter?

After I called Myron and told him I had decided to go to the dance I spent half of the next twenty-four hours in and out of the bathroom. It was certainly a local record and probably a national and international one too. I could see myself in the Guinness Book of World Records for Most Trips in One Day to the Bathroom Without Actually Doing Anything.

I hardly ate dinner. After showering I smoothed on a manly hair gel, splashed on a mentholly after-shave, and sprayed on a musky deodorant. I smelled muskmantholly magnificent. I almost got out of the house with my old sneakers, but my mom made me go back and put on my new slippery loafers.

My father drove Myron and me to the dance. "Break a leg," he yelled as I got out of the car.

"What's that all about?" asked Myron.

"Who knows," I replied. "Probably some weird expression he picked up when he was my age."

When we got to the gym steps, I scuffed the bottom of my new shoes to take away some of the slipperiness. The gym was decorated with blue and white streamers and red, white, and yellow balloons. At one end was a large sign picturing a boy and girl dancing. It said WELCOME, SEVENTH GRADERS. Tables with punch, cookies, pretzels, and potato chips lined both side walls. The bleachers were filled with boys and the dance floor was filled with girls.

Myron and I walked to the top of the bleachers and sat down. I would have been very happy sitting there all evening, but the teacher chaperons had a different agenda. Without any warning they went into the stands and shooed all of the boys out onto the floor. *Time to start acting,* I told myself.

Mr. Murray grabbed the microphone and said, "Girls make a circle." When they finished he said, "Boys make a circle around the girls' circle."

"Just what I wanted to do," I said to Myron. "Hold your hand and go around and around in a circle."

"When the music starts," instructed Mr. Murray, "I want the girls to circle clockwise and the boys to circle counterclockwise." The music started, and around both circles went. "When the music stops I want you to take the person in front of you for a partner."

Things were beginning to get serious. My heart was beating double time to the music and my musk-mantholly mist was turning to must. I secretly prayed for the song never to end. My prayer went unanswered and I found myself face to face with a girl—a tall girl—a very tall, muscular girl.

*Act calm,* I told myself. So what if her grandfather was Paul Bunyan. I smiled, she smiled back. I didn't know what to do next, so I smiled again.

"Introduce yourself to your partner," said Mr. Murray.

"I'm Elliot."

"I'm Paula."

Paula Bunyan, I thought. Should I ask if she has a pet ox at home? *Be calm, Elliot. Be Calm.*

"To get things warmed up," said Mr. Murray, "I thought we might start off with a Mexican hat dance. Cross your hands and take hold of your partner." My palms were soaking wet and I wiped them on my pants before I grabbed Paula's hands. "Left foot, right foot, left-right-left. Do that combination two times. Go." Even though I could tell everyone around me thought this was dumb, we all did it. I could tell my shoes were still a little slippery. "Now, with your hands still crossed, swing your partner around. Go." *Next thing he'll want us to do is a whole dance of this,* I thought. "Now I want you to put both steps together and do them in time to the music."

The music started and Paula jerked me toward her. The one good thing about this kind of dance was that we were still far enough away from each other that I didn't have to talk to her. With a little luck I'd be back in the stands watching in a few minutes.

"Left, right, left-right-left" barked Mr. Murray. "Left, right, left-right-left. . . . Now swing." Paula started off slowly, but as the music got louder she swung harder. The faster she swung, the dizzier I got. At the apex of the spin either she let go or my sweaty hands slipped away from hers. Either way I found myself spinning and twirling across the floor, straight for the punch bowl. The kids around us stopped to watch this whirling dervish. It seemed as if everyone was staring and pointing.

My left leg hit the table first, full force, causing it to tip forward. The strength of the blow caused my feet to slide out from under me and before I knew it I was on the ground and the table was on top of my legs. My pants were soaked with punch and my shirt was covered with smushed, smashed slivers of pretzels and potato chips.

There was almost complete silence until one of the kids started to laugh. Then everyone laughed. I felt stupid, dumb, and wet. I saw Mr. Murray running toward me to help, but Myron arrived first. I brushed myself off. He helped me up. I started to take a step, but my left leg refused to bear any weight and I collapsed in a heap.

The doctor at the hospital showed me the break in the X ray and told me my leg would be in a full leg cast for at least six weeks.

Since Myron came to the hospital with me, he was

the first to sign my cast. He laughed the whole time he was writing. When he finished he said, "Read it."

What he wrote started at my thigh and went down the entire length of the cast. It said, "Remember what your dad said to you when you got out of the car? I know you're supposed to listen to your parents, but this is ridiculous." I looked up at Myron, who was still smiling. "Your cast will be off just in time for the Thanksgiving Dance. Going?"

# About Joel Schwartz

●●●●●●●●

My first short story was written the first day of second grade. The title, "My Summer Vacation," was almost as long as the story. I did not begin seriously writing humorous stories for children and young adults until 1981, when I wrote my first novel, *Upchuck Summer*. Since then I have written five other novels, including *Best Friends Don't Come in Threes, Shrink, The Great Spaghetti Showdown, Upchuck Summer's Revenge,* and *Will the Nurse Make Me Take My Underwear Off and Other Mysteries of Life*.

I am married to my summer-camp sweetheart, Charlotte. We have a married son, Ron; a daughter-in-law, Lori; two daughters, Toby and Debby; and a Jack Russell terrier named Spencer. In my spare time I am a practicing child, adolescent, and adult psychiatrist and psychoanalyst. I am the associate medical director in charge of child and adolescent services at the Northwestern Institute in Fort Washington, Pennsylvania.

"Break a Leg" is based on an experience in dance class when I was thirteen. It is dedicated to all the kids in the class that year, with the exception of the girl who terrorized us. My most recent novel is *How to Get Rid of Your Older Brother,* a story of brotherly love. I was blackmailed into writing this by my younger brother. He always got away with murder!

To Virgil, being the frog boy
means a lot more than just
performing a role in a play.

• • • • • • • • • • •

# VIRGIL IS THE FROG BOY

## Constance Greene

**"I** am pleased to announce, class," said Mrs. Valenti, placing the tips of her fingers neatly together to make a church steeple, "that our fifth-grade play this year is to be that all-time favorite, *The Princess and the Frog Boy.*"

Virgil's heart went *boom boom boom* as it racketed around in his narrow chest. He didn't even hear the word "princess." All he heard was "the frog boy."

He raced home with the news.

"That the one where the frog turns into a handsome prince when the princess plants a big kiss on him?" Virgil's grandmother said.

Virgil didn't even hear the word "kiss." The only thing he heard was the word "frog."

"I hope I get it," Virgil said.

"You'd make a lovely frog boy, Virgie," said his grandmother. "I don't fancy you much as the princess, though."

He wished she wouldn't call him Virgie. Virgil was bad enough.

*Please, God,* Virgil prayed every night. *Please let me be the frog boy.* He got right down on his knees and everything. *Please God, just this once. I promise I won't ask for anything else if you'll just let me be the frog boy.*

"I'll never get it," Virgil said. "I know I won't."

"If they know their onions, they'll choose you," Virgil's grandmother said. "You'd be the best frog boy they could find, and I'm not saying that because you're my grandson. I'm saying it because it's true."

*I'll never get it. Never in a million, trillion years,* Virgil thought. *They'll pick Artie Macdougal. Artie always gets the good stuff. Wait and see. I'll never, ever get to be the frog boy.*

Virgil said the words over and over inside his head, figuring that if he said them often enough, he'd begin to believe them and when Artie was chosen to be frog boy, he, Virgil, wouldn't be so disappointed.

"Artie Macdougal will get it, you wait and see," Virgil told his friend Joe. "Artie always gets the good stuff."

He was right. Artie Macdougal got it. Everyone liked Artie Macdougal. Virgil liked Artie Macdougal. If only Artie didn't always get the good stuff.

"And class," Mrs. Valenti's voice rang out loud and clear, "I am pleased to announce our princess will be Bernadette Brophy."

Virgil and Joe and some others booed loudly.

"Class, please." Mrs. Valenti looked as if she had a stomachache. "Manners, please. We must remember our manners at all times."

Virgil knew all along that Bernadette Brophy would get to be the princess because Mrs. Valenti knew that if Bernadette didn't get to be princess, Bernadette would most likely blow Mrs. Valenti away, one way or another. Bernadette Brophy was a power person in the fifth grade. Bernadette had four brothers, all older than she was, and she had the biggest muscles in the family. People did what Bernadette Brophy wanted, or else. She told everyone these things and Virgil knew them to be true. Bernadette never told a lie. She didn't have to. The truth was spread out like a red carpet in front of Bernadette Brophy, waiting to be walked on.

Bernadette carried her pocketbook with her wherever she went, even when she was soccer goalie of the week. That pocketbook was plastic with the zipper gone. The faint smell of bitter almonds lingered in its folds and creases. That pocketbook was a terrible pale-yellow color, which reminded Virgil of frozen dog pee. In it Bernadette carried a bunch of old keys, which she said were for unlocking her secret trunks and stuff. Also in that pocketbook Bernadette carried a little tin of lip gloss in two flavors: cherry and butterscotch. Every day at recess Bernadette made a big deal of putting lip gloss on, then licking her lips and rolling her eyes and saying "yum yum," which drove some of the girls crazy.

And some of the boys too.

Bernadette had holes in her head. Well, actually, the

holes were in her ears, but Virgil called them holes in her head. The holes were plugged up with fourteen-karat gold. Earrings, that is. It even said 14 KARAT on the backs of the earrings, Bernadette said.

"Show me," scoffed Billy Boggs. "Oh, yeah. I'll believe that when you show me." Billy Boggs had a reputation as a tough guy because he said "Oh yeah, show me" quite a lot.

"I promised my mother I would never take these earrings off," Bernadette told Billy. She got away with murder, Bernadette did.

Sometimes Virgil had dreams of setting his giant Havahart trap and catching Bernadette in it. He never could remember what he'd used for bait, but it was only a dream and whenever he dreamed it, he woke up smiling.

"Maybe Artie'll die or get hit by lightning or something," Joe said, always the optimist.

"Nah. Artie never even gets sick," Virgil said. "He hasn't missed a day this year. Or last. I think he might've had chicken pox in second grade, but that's about it."

The next day Virgil's grandmother was waiting when he got home from school. "Try this on, Virgie," she said, holding out a mass of warty greenish brown cloth. "I finished it a little bit ago. See if it fits."

"What is it?" Virgil asked.

"A frog boy suit. What else?" his grandmother said. "Just in case."

"I told you, Grandmother." Virgil ran his fingers over the suit. "Artie Macdougal's the frog boy, not me."

"You never know, Virgie," his grandmother told him.

"It pays to be prepared. That's how we won the war, isn't it? I heard there was a case of scarlet fever over in Titusville. Maybe it's coming this way."

Virgil tried on the frog boy suit.

"Good, the feet fit," his grandmother said, smiling. "I wasn't too sure about those feet."

The feet fit perfectly.

"Turn, Virgie," said his grandmother. "I got to see it from all angles. Turn until I say stop."

Virgil turned until his head got dizzy and his knees got wobbly. "Can I stop turning now, please?" he said.

His grandmother sat back on her heels and said, "You look so handsome, Virgie. I think you should be the handsome prince, never mind the old frog boy."

Then she handed him a frog mask.

"Slip this on," she said. Virgil did. He looked at himself in the mirror and he liked what he saw.

*"Rivet,"* he croaked, as loud as he could. His grandmother jumped.

"That you, Virgie?" she said. "You sounded so real I thought a real frog got in here when I wasn't looking."

"Grandmother, would you please stop calling me Virgie?" Virgil said.

"Old habits die hard, Virgie," she said. "I'll try, but I can't promise anything."

*"Rivet, rivet,"* Virgil croaked, trying it on for size.

"What's 'rivet' mean anyway?" his grandmother asked.

"Maybe it means the frog's got a frog in his throat," Virgil said.

His grandmother didn't so much as smile, so he went to his bedroom and tucked his frog suit into his bottom drawer. If Artie Macdougal didn't get scarlet fever, he figured he could wear it on Halloween.

Next day, Mrs. Valenti was so charged up she couldn't sit still. She marched around the room carrying her blackboard pointer as if it were a sword. "This play might put us on the map, class," she said. "Think about it. This may be our big breakthrough."

"I thought we were already on the map," Virgil said.

Mrs. Valenti jabbed her pointer in his direction and snapped, "Attention. Come to order, class."

Rumor went around that there might be talent scouts in the audience the night *The Princess and the Frog Boy* opened. The scouts, it was said, were on the lookout for new talent for a big TV show.

Bernadette Brophy let it be known that even after she was offered a TV contract, her heart would be with her old buddies in her homeroom and after she got her limo, she promised she'd drive over and autograph her picture for a small fee.

Virgil kept a close eye on Artie Macdougal, who showed no signs of a rash or a fever. Artie's cheeks were rosy as the dawn and his eyes sparkled like the lake with the sun on it. Artie was in the pink.

"How's old Artie what's-his-name?" Virgil's grandmother asked daily.

"Never better," Virgil answered glumly.

Then, two days before *The Princess and the Frog Boy* was to open, Virgil found Artie Macdougal barfing his little brains out in the boys' room. Virgil's heart went *boom boom boom* as he held Artie's head and gave him a wad of paper towel to swab his face with.

Artie went home early, as wan and pale as any flu victim.

Bernadette went into a snit.

"What's his prob?" Bernadette demanded. "Doesn't he know the show must go on?"

In answer, Virgil let out a super-duper *rivet,* one which made the rafters ring and brought the school custodian on the double, thinking someone was up to no good. Virgil let loose a couple more *rivets,* and Bernadette ignored him.

"Artie Macdougal threw up in the boys' room today," Virgil told his grandmother when he got home.

"Poor little fella," she said, clapping her hands and doing a little dance. "Hope it's nothing serious."

It wasn't. Next day, there was Artie, good as new.

"You okay?" Virgil said in a trembly voice.

"Sure," Artie said. "Must've been those oysters. Oysters always make me sick."

Just when it seemed it never would, the big day arrived. The play was to start at six-thirty sharp. Before Virgil and his grandmother left the house he got down on his knees and gave it one last shot.

*Please, God,* he prayed. He was always careful to say "Please." *Please, God, I don't like to bug you, but this is Virgil. I would really like to be the frog boy just once. Just for a couple seconds is all.*

Sometimes God hears, only it takes a while for Him to come through. He's got quite a lot on his mind, after all.

Here's what happened:

The audience, made up of parents, grandparents, and a sprinkling of siblings who'd got their homework out of the way early, were gathered in the auditorium. Virgil and his grandmother got a seat way down front. After a lengthy wait for the play to begin, during which a fat, freckled fourth grader played a solo on the harmonica, the dusty red-plush curtains parted, revealing a remarkably real-looking forest. It looked to Virgil like the forest they'd used last year for Little Red Riding Hood, but he wasn't going to quibble. You seen one forest, you seen 'em all, was his motto.

The audience broke into applause, the forest looked so real. Loud giggles came from backstage and were loudly shushed. The lights were dimmed, the audience still.

*The Princess and the Frog Boy* was about to begin.

Bernadette Brophy floated on stage. The crowd gasped, she was so regal in her shimmery gown, carrying her shimmery wand. That wand was hoked up something fierce with sequins and things pasted onto it.

Then the frog boy shot into view, as if propelled from a cannon. Artie Macdougal stared out at the audience and Virgil was sure Artie was staring straight at him.

Virgil's grandmother rustled the brown paper bag she'd brought with her.

"What's that?" Virgil whispered.

"Your costume," his grandmother whispered back. "Just in case."

Virgil smiled sadly, thinking it took a lot to make her give up. His grandmother really hung in there, hoping for a miracle.

First crack out of the barrel, the princess, a.k.a. Bernadette Brophy, possessor of the best arm in the fifth grade, let fly with her glittery magic wand and nailed Artie Macdougal under his left ear, sending poor Artie to never-never land in one fell swoop.

With a gasp, the audience rose to its collective feet. Artie's mother fainted and Artie's father caught her with one smooth, practiced motion. Artie's mother fainted with some regularity, and Artie's father was used to catching her.

Smelling salts were called for. Bernadette's parents raced backstage to assess the damage, wondering out loud if perhaps a crisis counselor should be sent for immediately so that Bernadette wouldn't show scars of the event later in life.

Forget Bernadette. Artie's the guy should worry about scars.

"Hurry." Virgil's grandmother thrust the brown paper bag into Virgil's hands. "Get down low. Put it on. It's all set. All you have to do is get the feet on straight. The mask's on top. Hurry."

Virgil did as he was told. The audience was in a flap, wondering noisily what would happen now. Nobody noticed Virgil putting on his frog boy suit.

Bernadette had scragged Artie Macdougal as if it had been planned. If Bernadette and Virgil had been buddies, there might've been talk of a put-up job. They might say Bernadette had put Artie away on purpose. But Bernadette and Virgil were not, had never been, buddies.

Far from it.

Fate with a capital $F$ had intervened.

And not a breath of scandal could touch a hair on Virgil's head.

Not for nothing had Virgil practiced his leaps and croaks faithfully every night. Not for nothing had Virgil got down on his knees and asked God please to let him be the frog boy.

As Artie's inert form was hauled off the stage, feet first, Virgil, suited up and ready to go, whispered to himself, "I can do it, I can do it," much as the little engine had whispered "I think I can, I think I can."

A loud voice came from the audience. It said, "Get Virgil. Virgil's the frog boy! Get Virgil!"

Virgil felt his grandmother's hand push him out into the aisle.

"Get Virgil!" the voice came again.

Inside his frog mask, Virgil's face grew hot with embarrassment. Later, it was said by some that Virgil's grandmother had shouted those words, but there are always clinkers in every crowd.

Backstage, Mrs. Valenti was coming apart at the seams. She clapped her hands nervously and the dusty red-plush curtain began to close. The curtain pullers thought that's what the hand-clapping had signaled.

But they were wrong. Mrs. Valenti, who had once had theatrical ambitions of her own, said in a low and thrilling voice, "The show must go on."

And go on it did.

Without a backward glance, without a second thought, Virgil jumped into the role of the frog boy as if he'd been born to play it. It was like something out of one of those old movies where the loser, the little guy on the bottom rung of the ladder, suddenly comes to life and winds up a star, his name in lights.

That was what happened.

Up there on the stage, leaping and croaking his heart out, Virgil *was* the frog boy. His costume was perfect. He looked as real as the forest. His mask was so life-like, it made little children think twice.

As Virgil gazed out over the footlights through his bulgy frog eyes and breathed through his curly little frog mouth, he knew that never in his entire life had he been as happy as he was at this moment. It was something he'd remember all of his days.

Every time Bernadette waved her magic wand, Virgil ducked. Bernadette was fast on her feet, but Virgil was faster. Scarcely out of breath, Virgil leaped and ducked and croaked as if his very life depended on it. Which, in a way, it did.

At the end, the audience gave the cast a standing ovation.

"Bravo, Virgil!" the voice shouted, the same voice that had shouted "Get Virgil!"

"Bravo, Virgil!" the voice shouted.

The crowd took up the cry.

"Bravo, Virgil! Bravo!"

Bernadette took two bows to every one of Virgil's. Every time a Bravo! rang out, Bernadette dipped her head modestly and sank low in a curtsy that brought her nose to within sniffing distance of the stage. Time after time, Bernadette swung her mighty arm. If Virgil hadn't been such a good ducker, she would've nailed him the way she'd nailed poor Artie Macdougal.

From there on, Virgil was known as the frog boy.

Frog, for short.

"In your other life, Virgie," his grandmother said, folding the frog boy suit neatly before packing it away in moth balls, "I think maybe you really *were* a frog." Virgil's grandmother had once studied to be a before- and afterlife counselor, and knew about such things.

Virgil looked at himself long and hard in the mirror. Even when he bugged out his eyes, he didn't think he looked too much like a frog. Although he rather liked the idea.

*"Rivet,"* he croaked, just to keep in shape. *"Rivet, rivet."*

The sound echoed and bounced against the walls.

"I thought I heard you talking," Joe said. "Here." He handed Virgil a jar full of flies, bouncing and bumping against the glass, wanting out. "It's a present for you."

"It isn't even my birthday or anything," Virgil said.

"Hey, I saved 'em for you," Joe said. "Frogs eat flies, don't they?"

# About Constance Greene

• • • • • • • •

I like writing books for children and feel lucky that it seems to be what I do best. Children keep on growing and are replaced with still more, and different, children. My audience is constantly being replenished, which is nice.

When I wrote my first book, *A Girl Called Al*, my house was still filled with children. The two oldest were in college, but the other three were at home. They provided me with much material, for which I was not ungrateful—but then, I figured they owed me. After all those egg salad sandwiches, it was the least they could do.

Now my children have children of their own. My grandchildren keep me posted as to what's current. Dress, slang, others. God forbid I should not be current. As a writer of "contemporary" books for kids, it is essential to know what goes on without becoming trendy, thereby dating the book.

Children want to know which of my books is my favorite. I tell them *A Girl Called Al* is a favorite because she was my first character; and I like her so much, I've written five sequels to her. And *Beat the Turtle Drum* is a favorite because it is the most autobiographical of my books. And *The Love Letters Of J. Timothy Owen* is another favorite because it was so much fun to write. Everything fell into place in that book and the finished product delights me, makes me laugh.

VIRGIL IS THE FROG BOY. These words are written on a bridge overpass near where I live. I like those words, they speak to me. I knew some day I would use them. Virgil is a good name. Who was Virgil and why was he the frog boy? I wrote the short story with the idea of possibly using it at some later date in a book about Virgil. I can see him in my mind's eye. He clamors for more attention. I plan to give it to him.

At the moment, I am finishing a funny book for boys, age seven to ten. Boys, it seems, are much more reluctant to read than girls. If you can make them laugh, legend has it, you've got them for life.

I hope this works.

I am also working on a book about two sisters whose widowed father is thinking of marrying a woman they hate. They do everything in their power to prevent the marriage.

I do not know if they are successful. Time will tell.

Lucas has always been the class clown,
but his latest prank gives him
more than he's bargained for.

• • • • • • • • • •

# RABBITS

## Johanna Hurwitz

**I**t was time for phys. ed.
Lucas Cott jumped from his seat and lined up with his
classmates. If he had to sit at his desk one more minute, he would explode. Thank goodness he could escape to the gym.

"Lucas Cott. Where do you think you are going?"

It was the voice of his teacher, Mrs. Hockaday.

"I'm going to phys. ed. That's what it says on our
schedule," said Lucas, pointing to the chalkboard
where the plan for the day was outlined.

"That schedule is for students who don't cause trouble. You have been a nuisance from the moment you
walked in the door this morning. You've been clowning
around and creating a disturbance. Mr. Lyons, the

phys. ed. teacher, told me you did the same thing in the gym last week. I think you need a little quiet time to think about the proper way to behave in school."

"I think about it," said Lucas. "Sometimes. When I'm not thinking about arithmetic and spelling and lunch. There are an awful lot of things to think about at school," he complained. "I can't think about everything at the same time."

"Well, now you can think and you can write," said Mrs. Hockaday. She handed Lucas a piece of lined paper. "I want you to write *I must behave properly in class,* fifty times."

"Now?" said Lucas.

"Right now!" said Mrs. Hockaday. "Go back to your seat and begin at once."

So while everyone else in the class was in phys. ed., Lucas was alone in the classroom with Mrs. Hockaday.

"Lucas, you have to learn that there are consequences to your actions," Mrs. Hockaday informed her student.

Lucas thought about his classmates all having a great time playing volleyball. And there he was stuck in his seat, writing. He would never finish this awful assignment.

*I must behave properly in class,* he wrote across the top of the page. He looked at the clock in the front of the room. It took thirty-five seconds to write those words. If it took that long to write it once, it would take fifty times thirty-five seconds to write it out fifty times. Lucas turned the paper over to the other side to figure it out.

$$\begin{array}{r} 50 \\ \times\,35 \\ \hline 250 \\ 150\phantom{0} \\ \hline 1750 \end{array}$$

1,750 seconds! Wow. Then Lucas had to divide all those seconds by sixty to figure out how many minutes it would take him to write out *I must behave properly in class*, fifty times.

Before he got the answer, Mrs. Hockaday was standing over him.

"Lucas Cott! Why are you doing arithmetic now? I gave you work to do and that's what you should be doing."

Lucas sighed and turned his paper over. It probably was better not to know how many hours it would take him to finish this job. He started writing again.

> *I must behave properly in class.*
> *I must behave properly in class*
> *I*
> *I*
> *I*

It was very boring, and at the rate he was going Lucas was afraid he would have to take the paper home and finish the task that evening. Lucas didn't want to do that, but he didn't want to write out the sentences either. His fingers ached from holding the pencil and his neck was getting stiff from staring down at the paper for such a long time.

Lucas looked up at the clock. There were another

twenty minutes until his classmates were due to return from the gym.

Lucas saw that Mrs. Hockaday was watching him. "I have to go to the office for a couple of minutes," she told Lucas. "You have plenty to keep you busy. I expect to find you sitting in your seat and writing when I return."

With those words, the teacher got up from her desk and walked out of the room.

Lucas let out a sigh and wrote two more *I*'s on the page. He listened as his teacher's footsteps went farther and farther down the hallway. As soon as he felt she was a distance away, he put down his pencil and stood up to stretch his legs. He walked around the classroom and punched an imaginary volleyball over an imaginary net with his fist.

If he had had a ball, it would have landed right on top of the cage in the back of the classroom. The cage held the newest member of Lucas's class. He was a large white rabbit named Bernard Whiskers. Lucas walked to the back of the room and stuck his finger through the mesh wires. He stroked Bernard's soft fur.

"You're just like me," said Lucas sympathetically to the rabbit. "You're locked in and all alone too."

Unlike Lucas, Bernard Whiskers was always silent. No matter how bored or restless the rabbit was, his mouth never made a sound. His little feet with his long nails might scratch among the shredded newspapers that lined the cage. Or he might crunch away on a lettuce leaf or a piece of carrot, but he made no other noise.

"I bet you'd like to play with Floppy Ears," said Lucas to Bernard.

Bernard Whiskers made no response except to chew on a piece of wilted lettuce inside his cage.

Floppy Ears was the rabbit that lived in Mrs. Van Zuuk's second-grade classroom next door. Only two classes in the school were lucky enough to have pet rabbits. Lucas remembered that the second graders had gone on a trip to the local fire station. He had gone on that trip back when he was in second grade.

Lucas stuck his head out the classroom door. There was no one in the hallway. Did he dare? Of course he did. He went outside into the hall and then into Mrs. Van Zuuk's classroom. No one was there except Floppy Ears, who was lying quietly on the floor of his cage.

"Wake up, Floppy Ears," said Lucas. "How would you like a chance to visit with Bernard Whiskers?"

Floppy Ears did not pay any attention to Lucas. But when Lucas opened the latch on his cage, Floppy Ears stood up.

Lucas took the brown rabbit out of the cage and carried him into his classroom. He opened the door to Bernard Whiskers's cage and put Floppy Ears inside.

"Now, play nicely," instructed Lucas. "No fighting and be sure to share your lettuce and carrots," he told Bernard Whiskers.

Just then, Lucas heard the click of Mrs. Hockaday's high heel shoes walking on the linoleum out in the hallway. Lucas hadn't expected his teacher to return so soon. Quickly, he latched the rabbit cage shut and rushed back to his seat. He grabbed his pencil and managed to write

*must*

*must*

*must*

on his sheet of paper before the teacher entered the classroom.

"I am glad to see you are working," said Mrs. Hockaday. "If you would only learn to control your tongue, life would be much easier for you."

Lucas licked his lips with his tongue. He liked his tongue just as it was. Besides, it wasn't his tongue that did the talking. It was his whole mouth working together. He had once spent an entire lunch hour conversing with his friends Julio and Franklin without moving his tongue at all. The sounds that had come out were not all recognizable, but the boys had thought it was very funny.

Mrs. Hockaday didn't notice that Floppy Ears was visiting inside of Bernard Whiskers's cage. Lucas wondered what she would say if she did. He planned to return Floppy Ears to the second-grade class when his teacher went to get his classmates at the end of phys. ed. time.

Unfortunately, Mrs. Hockaday insisted that Lucas accompany her when she walked to the gymnasium.

"Can't I stay here and finish my work?" asked Lucas. He still had a lot of lines to write.

"No. Come along with me," said Mrs. Hockaday. So Lucas was forced to follow his teacher down the hallway and miss the chance to remove Floppy Ears from

Bernard Whiskers's cage. That probably was fine with the two rabbits, but Lucas began to worry when he would have another opportunity. Just as Lucas and his classmates were returning from the gym, three loud gongs sounded.

"A fire drill. A fire drill," Lucas called out with delight.

Fire drills were wonderful for wasting time. By the time the drill was over it would be lunchtime!

Doors opened all along the corridor and classes lined up with their teachers, ready to leave the building. Lucas and his classmates marched along the hallway. Students waved to their friends in the other classes. "The second grade is missing the fire drill," Lucas observed to Cricket Kaufman, who was standing beside him. "They went to the fire station. Isn't that funny to be at the fire station while we're having a fire drill?"

Cricket didn't respond. It was against school rules to speak during a fire drill and Cricket never broke a rule. She turned her head away from Lucas. She did not want to be contaminated by his bad behavior.

The students marched outside the building and stood in their designated areas. Mrs. Hockaday walked up and down the rows of students, counting heads. "Everyone is here." She nodded.

It was chilly outside and some of the girls were holding their arms around themselves and jumping up and down to keep warm. Mrs. Hockaday was wearing her open-toed shoes today. Lucas wondered if her toes were cold. But even though he could feel the cold air through his flannel shirt, Lucas pretended that he was hot. He opened a couple of buttons on his shirt and pretended to fan himself from the hot air. Some of the other boys noticed and they copied him. Soon half the third grade was standing with open shirts and waving their arms in the air.

"Lucas. Button up your shirt," scolded Mrs. Hockaday. "Do you want to get pneumonia?"

"If it's so cold outside, why did they make a fire drill?" Lucas asked his teacher. And then a glorious idea came to him. "Hey. Maybe this isn't a drill. Maybe the school really is on fire."

He sniffed deeply, hoping to smell smoke. But at the very next moment the three gongs that meant return to your classrooms sounded. The school wasn't burning down after all, and everyone had to go back inside.

Now it was lunchtime and in the rush of getting lunch boxes and hurrying off to eat, no one noticed that Bernard Whiskers and Floppy Ears were eating their lunch together today. Lucas was so busy rushing off to lunch that he quite forgot about what he had done earlier.

Franklin's mother had given him celery sticks in his lunch box. Franklin hated celery, but he always asked his mother for it just the same. He put the sticks in his shirt pocket and when the children returned to the classroom after lunch, he went to give Bernard Whiskers a treat. That's what he always did with his celery.

"Hey, look at this," he shouted to his classmates and to the teacher.

Everyone turned to look in the direction of the rabbit cage.

"There are two rabbits in here," Franklin announced.

"That's Floppy Ears," said Cricket Kaufman, recognizing the intruder. "How did he get in there?"

Everyone in the class crowded around the rabbit cage to look at the pair of occupants. Lucas stood next to Cricket and for once in his life, he kept silent. He wasn't sure what Mrs. Hockaday would do if she knew he was responsible. He decided that unless he was asked a direct question about the affair, he would say nothing. Mrs. Hockaday seemed to have forgotten that Lucas had been alone in the room earlier.

"This is most peculiar," said the teacher. "The second graders will be worrying about their pet. Franklin, take him back to their classroom where he belongs, at once."

Franklin proudly unlatched the cage and removed Floppy Ears. He slipped a couple of his celery sticks into the cage for Bernard Whiskers as a consolation prize for the rabbit, who would now be alone again. And he kept a couple of other pieces of his celery for Floppy Ears.

"All right, everyone," said Mrs. Hockaday. "In your seats and take out your books. It is time for silent reading."

Some weeks later, it was not Franklin but Sara Jane Cushman, who usually was as quiet as a rabbit herself, who startled everyone by calling out, "Look. Look at Bernard Whiskers."

The white rabbit was lying on the floor of his cage. And with him were five tiny baby rabbits. The babies were the size of one of Lucas's fingers. They had no hair and hardly looked like rabbits at all.

"Bernard is a father," said Julio in amazement.

"Bernard Whiskers is a mother rabbit," said Cricket Kaufman. She was the class brain and could figure things out faster than just about anyone else.

The class quickly voted to change Bernard's name to Beatrix Whiskers.

No one ever knew that it was Lucas who was responsible for the increased rabbit population at the school. Of course, Lucas figured it out quickly enough. Like Cricket, he was pretty smart too. If Mrs. Hockaday ever suspected Lucas's role in the affair, she never mentioned it, which was just as well. Lucas was afraid he would have been made to write *I must not play with the rabbits* about five hundred times, if she knew what he had done.

It was certainly the worst piece of mischief that Lucas had pulled off all year, even if it was the most quiet. Yet in a way it was the best thing he had done too. It made him start thinking about the fact that one's behavior sometimes can have results and reactions that one doesn't expect. And if that is the case, perhaps one ought to think before one acted. It was something new for Lucas to consider. It was what Mrs. Hockaday had been trying to make him understand all year.

In a few weeks, five other classrooms in the school had cages with rabbits in them too. The rabbits were brown and white and were named Flopsy, Mopsy, Cottontail, Peter, and Bernard Whiskers II. No one was sure if the names were appropriate to the sex of the rabbits.

Some days, when Lucas wasn't too busy with his arithmetic or spelling or phys. ed. or lunch, he wondered about the possibility of introducing the various other animals that lived in the school building to one another. There were frogs in terrariums in a couple of classrooms, several aquariums filled with fish, and a lone tortoise in the kindergarten room. Wouldn't it be wonderful if all these creatures could begin reproducing. Soon the school would be filled with fish and animals. It would be more like a zoo than a school then. Lucas wondered if he could arrange that. It would be super.

# About Johanna Hurwitz

• • • • • • • •

I have written over thirty books for boys and girls. Among them are *The Adventures of Ali Baba Bernstein, Baseball Fever, The Hot and Cold Summer, Rip-Roaring Russell,* and the books about Aldo Sossi and his family. In addition to my books of fiction, I have also written biographies of Anne Frank and Astrid Lindgren. At present, I am working on a biography of the late composer/ conductor Leonard Bernstein.

Over the years, some of my books have been designated Notable Books by the American Library Association. Two books were selected as Parents Choice winners. But the prizes I am most proud of are those awards that are voted for by my readers. My books have won the Children's Choice award in several states.

Perhaps when you are reading "Rabbits" you will recognize the mischief-maker in the story. He is the same Lucas Cott who appeared in my books *Class Clown, Teacher's Pet, Class President,* and *School's Out.* Lucas was such a champion at misbehaving that I couldn't tell everything about him in *Class Clown.* I knew of many other escapades he had gotten into. I was glad of this chance to pass along still another of his pranks. Nowadays, Lucas Cott is getting ready to appear in a future book of mine.

Is Paul a born storyteller . . .
or just a liar?

• • • • • • • • • •

# THE AUTHOR

## M. E. Kerr

**B**efore the author comes to school, we all have to write him, saying we are glad he is coming and we like his books.

That is Ms. Terripelli's idea. She is our English teacher and she was the one who first got the idea to have real, live authors visit Leighton Middle School.

She wants the author to feel welcome.

*You are my favorite author,* I write.

I have never read anything he's written.

*Please send me an autographed picture,* I write. I am sure this will raise my English grade, something I need desperately, since it is not one of my best subjects.

The truth is: I have best friends and best clothes and best times, but not best subjects.

*I am going to be an author, too, someday,* I write,

surprised to see the words pop up on the screen. But I am writing on the computer in the school library and there is something wonderful about the way any old thought can become little green letters in seconds, which you can erase with one touch of your finger.

I don't push WordEraser, however.

I like writing that I am going to be an author.

The person I am writing to is Peter Sand.

My name happens to be Peter too.

Peter Sangetti.

*I might shorten my name to Peter Sang, when I become an author,* I write. *Then maybe people will buy my books by mistake, thinking they are getting yours. (Ha! Ha!)*

*Well,* I write, *before this turns into a book and you sell it for money, I will sign off, but I will be looking for you when you show up at our school.*

I sign it *Sincerely,* although that's not exactly true.

The night before the author visit, my dad comes over to see me. My stepfather and my mother have gone off to see my stepbrother, Tom, in Leighton High School's version of *The Sound of Music.*

To myself, and sometimes to my mother, I call him Tom Terrific. Naturally, he has the lead in the musical. He is Captain Von Trapp. If they ever make the Bible into a play, he will be God.

I like him all right, but I am tired of playing second fiddle to him always. He is older, smarter, and better looking, and his last name is Prince. Really.

I can't compete with him.

It's funny, because the first words out of my dad's mouth that night are, "I can't compete with that."

He is admiring the new CD audio system my stepfather had ordered from the Sharper Image catalog. It is an Aiwa with built-in BBE sound.

"It's really for Tom Terrific," I say, but it is in the living room, not Tom's bedroom, and Dad knows my CD collection is my pride and joy.

I suppose just as I try to compete with Tom Terrific, my dad tries to compete with Thomas Prince, Sr. . . . Both of us are losing the game, it seems. My dad is even out of work just now, although it is our secret . . . not to be shared with my mom or stepfather.

The plant where he worked was closed. He'd have to move out of the state to find the same kind of job he had there, and he doesn't want to leave me.

"I'm not worried about you," I lie. And then I hurry to change the subject, and tell him about the author's visit, next day.

He smiles and shakes his head. "Funny. I once wanted to be a writer."

"I never knew that."

"Sure. One time I got this idea for a story about our cat. She was always sitting in the window of our apartment building, looking out. She could never get out, but she'd sit there, and I'd think it'd be her dream come true if she could see a little of the world! Know what I mean, Pete?"

"Sure I do." I also know my dad always wished he could travel. He is the only person I've ever known who actually reads *National Geographic*.

He laughs. "So I invented a story about the day she got out. Here was her big chance to run around the block!"

"What happened?"

"A paper bag fell from one of the apartments above ours. It landed right on Petunia's head. She ran around the block, all right, but she didn't see a thing."

Both of us roar at the idea, but deep down I don't think it is that hilarious, considering it is my dad who dreamed it up.

What's he think—that he'll never see the world? Never have his dreams come true?

"Hey, what's the matter?" he says. "You look down in the dumps suddenly."

"Not me," I say.

"Aw, that was a dumb story," he says. "Stupid!"

"It was fine," I say.

"No, it wasn't," he says. "I come over here and say things to spoil your evening. You'd rather hear your music."

"No, I wouldn't," I say, but he is getting up to go.

We are losing touch not living in the same house anymore.

Whenever I go over to his apartment, he spends a lot of time apologizing for it. It is too small. It isn't very cheerful. It needs a woman's touch. I want to tell him that if he'd just stop pointing out all the things wrong with it, I'd like it fine . . . but it is turning out that we aren't great talkers anymore. I don't say everything on my mind anymore.

He shoots me a mock punch at the door and tells me

that next week he'll get some tickets to a hockey game. Okay with me? I say he doesn't have to, thinking of the money, and he says I know it's not like going to the World Series or anything. I'd gone to the World Series the year before with my stepfather.

"Let up," I mumble.

"What?" he says.

"Nothing."

He says, "I heard you, Pete. You're right. You're right."

Next day, waiting for me out front is Ms. Terripelli.

"He asked for you, Pete! You're going to be Mr. Sand's guide for the day."

"Why me?" I ask.

"Because you want to be a writer?" She looks at me and I look at her.

"Oh, that," I say.

"You never told the class that," she says.

"It's too personal."

"Do you write in secret, Pete?"

"I have a lot of ideas," I say.

"Good for you!" says Ms. Terripelli, and she hands me a photograph of Peter Sand. It is autographed. It also has written on it, "Maybe someday I'll be asking for yours, so don't change your name. Make me wish it was mine, instead."

"What does all that mean?" Ms. Terripelli asks me.

"Just author stuff," I say.

I put the picture in my locker and go to the faculty lounge to meet him.

He is short and plump, with a mustache. He looks

like a little colonel of some sort, because he has this booming voice and a way about him that makes you feel he knows his stuff.

"I never write fantasy," he says. "I write close to home. When you read my books, you're reading about something that happened to me! . . . Some authors write both fantasy and reality!"

At the end of his talks he answers all these questions about his books and he autographs paperback copies.

I hang out with him the whole time.

We don't get to say much to each other until lunch.

The school doesn't dare serve him what we get in the cafeteria, so they send out for heros, and set up a little party for him in the lounge.

The principal shows up, and some librarians from the Leighton Town Library.

When we do get a few minutes to talk he asks me what I am writing.

I say, "We had this cat, Petunia, who was always looking out the window . . ."

He is looking right into my eyes as though he is fascinated, and I finish the story.

"Wow!" he says. "Wow!"

"It's sort of sad," I say.

"It has heart and it has humor, Pete," he says. "The best stories always do."

His last session is in the school library, and members of the town are invited.

About fifty people show up.

He talks about his books for a while, and then he starts talking about me.

He tells the story about Petunia. He called it wistful and amusing, and he says anyone who can think up a story like that knows a lot about the world already.

I get a lot of pats on the back afterward, and Ms. Terripelli says, "Well, you've had quite a day for yourself, Pete."

By this time I am having trouble looking her in the eye.

Things are a little out of hand, but what the heck— he is on his way to the airport and back to Maine, where he lives. What did it hurt that I told a few fibs?

Next day, the *Leighton Lamplighter* has the whole story. I hadn't even known there was a reporter present. There is the same photograph Peter Sand has given to me, and there is my name in the article about the author visit.

My name. Dad's story of Petunia, with no mention of Dad.

"Neat story!" says Tom Terrific.

My stepfather says if I show him a short story all finished and ready to send out somewhere, he'll think about getting me a word processor.

"I don't write for gain," I say.

Mom giggles. "You're a wiseguy, Pete."

"Among other things," I say.

Like a liar, I am thinking. Like a liar and a cheat.

When Dad calls, I am waiting for the tirade.

He has a bad temper. He is the type who leaves

nothing unsaid when he blows. I expect him to blow blue: he does when he loses his temper. He comes up with slang that would knock the socks off the Marine Corps.

"Hey, Pete," he says, "you really liked my story, didn't you?"

"Too much, I guess. That's why you didn't get any credit."

"What's mine is yours, kid. I've always told you that."

"I went off the deep end, I guess, telling him I want to be a writer."

"An apple never falls far from the tree, Pete. That was my ambition when I was your age."

"Yeah, you told me. . . . But *me*. What do I know?"

"You have a good imagination, son. And you convinced Peter Sand what you were saying was true."

"I'm a good liar, I guess."

"Or a good storyteller. . . . Which one?"

Why does he have to say which one?

Why does he have to act so pleased to have given me something?

The story of Petunia isn't really a gift. I realize that now. It was more like a loan.

I can tell the story, just as my dad told it to me, but when I try to turn myself from a liar into a storyteller, it doesn't work on paper.

I fool around with it for a while. I try.

The thing is: fantasy is not for me.

I finally find out what is when I come up with a first sentence which begins:

# FUNNY YOU SHOULD ASK

*Before the author comes to school, we all have to write him, saying we are glad he is coming and we like his books.*

You see, I am an author who writes close to home.

# About M. E. Kerr

• • • • • • • •

M. E. Kerr is the pen name of Marijane Meaker, who has been writing for children and young adults since 1972, when *Dinky Hocker Shoots Smack!* was published. Since then, she has written fifteen more books, including *Is That You, Miss Blue?; Gentlehands; Little, Little; Night Kites;* and *Fell.* Her autobiography is called *Me Me Me Me Me: Not a Novel.* Her most recent book, written under the pen name Mary James, is *Shoebag,* about a cockroach who turns into a little boy.

M. E. Kerr was born in Auburn, New York. She attended the University of Missouri and now lives in East Hampton on Long Island, New York.

Robert knows that he'd better not forget
his lines, or Belinda Lopez will *kill* him.

• • • • • • • • • • •

# THE SCHOOL PLAY

## Gary Soto

**I**n the school play at the
end of his sixth-grade year, all Robert Suarez had to
remember to say was, "Nothing's wrong, I can see," to
a pioneer woman, who was really Belinda Lopez. Instead of a pioneer woman, Belinda was one of the
toughest girls since the beginning of the world. She
was known to slap boys and grind their faces into the
grass so that they bit into chunks of wormy earth.
More than once Robert had witnessed Belinda staring
down the janitor's pit bull, who licked his frothing
chops but didn't dare mess with her.

The class rehearsed for three weeks, at first without
costumes. Early one morning Mrs. Bunnin wobbled
into the classroom lugging a large cardboard box. She

wiped her brow and said, "Thanks for the help, Robert."

Robert was at his desk scribbling a ballpoint tattoo that spelled DUDE on the tops of his knuckles. He looked up and stared, blinking at his teacher. "Oh, did you need some help?" he asked.

She rolled her eyes at him and told him to stop writing on his skin. "You'll look like a criminal," she scolded.

Robert stuffed his hands into his pockets as he rose from his seat. "What's in the box?" he asked.

She muttered under her breath. She popped open the Scotch-taped top and brought out skirts, hats, snow shoes, scarves, and vests. She tossed Robert a red beard, which he held up to his face, thinking it made him look handsome.

"I like it," Robert said. He sneezed and ran his hand across his moist nose.

His classmates were coming into the classroom and looked at Robert in awe. "That's bad," Ruben said. "What do I get?"

Mrs. Bunnin threw him a wrinkled shirt. Ruben raised it to his chest and said, "My dad could wear this. Can I give it to him after the play is done?"

Mrs. Bunnin turned away in silence.

Most of the actors didn't have speaking parts. They just got cutout crepe-paper snowflakes to pin to their shirts or crepe-paper leaves to wear.

During the blizzard in which Robert delivered his line, Belinda asked, "Is there something wrong with your eyes?" Robert looked at the audience, which at the moment was a classroom of empty chairs, a dented world globe that had been dropped by almost everyone, one limp flag, one wastebasket, and a picture of George Washington, whose eyes followed you around the room when you got up to sharpen your pencil. Robert answered, "Nothing's wrong. I can see."

Mrs. Bunnin, biting on the end of her pencil, said, "Louder, both of you."

Belinda stepped up, nostrils flaring so that the shadows on her nose quivered, and said louder, "Sucka, is there something wrong with your eyeballs?"

"Nothing's wrong. I can see."

"Louder! Make sure the audience can hear you," Mrs. Bunnin directed. She tapped her pencil hard against the desk. She scolded, "Robert, I'm not going to tell you again to quit fooling with the beard."

"It's itchy."

"We can't do anything about that. Actors need props. You're an actor. Now try again."

Robert and Belinda stood center stage as they waited for Mrs. Bunnin to call "action!" When she did, Belinda approached Robert slowly. "Sucka face, is there anything wrong with your mug?" Belinda asked. Her eyes were squinted in anger. For a moment Robert saw his head grinding into the playground grass.

"Nothing's wrong. I can see."

Robert giggled behind his red beard. Belinda popped her gum and smirked. She stood with her hands on her hips.

"What? What did you say?" Mrs. Bunnin asked, pulling off her glasses. "Are you chewing gum, Belinda?"

"No, Mrs. Bunnin," Belinda lied. "I just forgot my lines."

Belinda turned to face the snowflake boys clumped together in the back. She rolled out her tongue on which rested a ball of gray gum, depleted of sweetness under her relentless chomp. She whispered "sucka," and giggled so that her nose quivered dark shadows.

The play, *The Last Stand,* was about the Donner party just before they got hungry and started eating each other. Everyone who scored at least twelve out of fifteen on their spelling tests got to say at least one line. Everyone else had to stand and be trees or snowflakes.

Mrs. Bunnin wanted the play to be a success. She couldn't risk having kids with bad memories on stage. The nonspeaking trees and snowflakes stood humming snow flurries, blistering wind, and hail, which they produced by clacking their teeth.

Robert's mother was proud of him because he was living up to the legend of Robert De Niro, for whom he was named. Over dinner he said, "Nothing's wrong. I can see," when his brother asked him to pass the dish towel, their communal napkin. His sister said, "It's your turn to do dishes," and he said, "Nothing's wrong. I can see." His dog, Queenie, begged him for more than water and a Milk-Bone. He touched his dog's own hairy beard and said, "Nothing's wrong. I can see."

One warm spring night, Robert lay on his back in the backyard, counting shooting stars. He was up to three when David, a friend who was really his brother's friend, hopped the fence and asked, "What's the matter with you?"

"Nothing's wrong. I can see," Robert answered. He sat up, feeling good because the line came naturally, without much thought. He leaned back on his elbow and asked David what he wanted to be when he grew up.

"I don't know yet," David said, plucking at the grass. "Maybe a fighter pilot. What do you want to be?"

"I want to guard the president. I could wrestle the assassins, and be on television. But I'd pin those dudes and people would say, 'That's him, our hero.' " David plucked at stalk of grass and thought deeply.

Robert thought of telling David that he really wanted to be someone with a supergreat memory, who could recall facts that most people thought were unimportant. He didn't know if there was such a job, but he thought it would be great to sit at home by the telephone waiting for scientists to call him and ask hard questions.

The three weeks passed quickly. The day before the play, Robert felt happy as he walked home from school with no homework. As he turned onto his street, he found a dollar floating over the currents of wind.

"A buck," he screamed to himself. He snapped it up and looked for others. But he didn't find any more. It was his lucky day, though. At recess he had hit a home run on a fluke bunt—a fluke because the catcher had kicked the ball, another player had thrown it into center field, and the pitcher wasn't looking when Robert slowed down at third, then burst home with dust flying behind him.

That night, it was his sister's turn to do the dishes. They had eaten enchiladas with the works, so she slaved with suds up to her elbows. Robert bathed in

Mr. Bubble, the suds peaked high like the Donner Pass. He thought about how full he was, and how those poor people had had nothing to eat but snow. I can live on nothing, he thought, and whistled like wind through a mountain pass, raking flat the Mr. Bubble suds with his palm.

The next day, after lunch, he was ready for the play, red beard in hand, and his one line trembling on his lips. Classes herded into the auditorium. As the actors dressed and argued about stepping on each other's feet, Robert stood near a cardboard barrel full of toys, whispering over and over to himself, "Nothing's wrong. I can see." He was hot, itchy, and confused when he tied on the beard. He sneezed when a strand of the beard entered his nostril. He said louder, "Nothing's wrong. I can see," but the words seemed to get caught in the beard. "Nothing, no, no. I can see great," he said louder, then under his breath because the words seemed wrong. "Nothing's wrong, can't you see? Nothing's wrong. I can see you." Worried, he approached Belinda and asked if she remembered his line. Balling her hand into a fist, Belinda warned, "Sucka, I'm gonna bury your ugly face in the ground if you mess up."

"I won't," Robert said as he walked away. He bit a nail and looked into the barrel of toys. A clown's mask stared back at him. He prayed that his line would come back to him. He would hate to disappoint his teacher and didn't like the thought of his face being rubbed into spiky grass.

The curtain parted slightly and the principal came out smiling onto the stage. She said some words about pioneer history and then, stern-faced, warned the audience not to scrape the chairs on the just-waxed floor. The principal then introduced Mrs. Bunnin, who told the audience about how they had rehearsed for weeks.

Meanwhile, the class stood quietly in place with lunchtime spaghetti on their breath. They were ready. Belinda had swallowed her gum because she knew this was for real. The snowflakes clumped together and began howling.

Robert retied his beard. Belinda, smoothing her skirt, looked at him and said, "If you know what's good for you, you'd better do it right." Robert grew nervous when the curtain parted, and his classmates, who were assigned to do snow, wind, and hail, broke into song.

Alfonso stepped forward with his narrative about a blot on American history that would live with us forever. He looked at the audience, lost for a minute. He continued by saying that if the Donner party could come back, hungry from not eating for over a hundred years, they would be sorry for what they had done.

The play began with some boys in snowshoes shuffling around the stage, muttering that the blizzard would cut them off from civilization. They looked up, held out their hands, and said in unison, "Snow." One stepped center stage and said, "I wish I had never left the prairie." Another one said, "California is just over there." He pointed, and some of the first graders looked in the direction of the piano.

"What are we going to do?" one kid asked, brushing pretend snow off his vest.

"I'm getting pretty hungry," another said, rubbing her stomach.

The audience seemed to be following the play. A

ribbon of sweat ran down Robert's face. When his scene came up he staggered to center stage and dropped to the floor, just as Mrs. Bunnin had said, just as he had seen Robert De Niro do in that movie about a boxer. Belinda, bending over with an "Oh, my," yanked him up so hard that something clicked in his elbow. She boomed, "Is there anything wrong with your eyes?"

Robert rubbed his elbow, then his eyes, and said, "I can see nothing wrong. Wrong is nothing, I can see."

"How are we going to get through?" she boomed, wringing her hands together at the audience, some of whom had their mouths taped shut because they were known talkers. "My husband needs a doctor." The drama advanced through snow, wind, and hail that sounded like chattering teeth.

Belinda turned to Robert and muttered, "You mess-up. You're gonna hate life."

But Robert thought he'd done okay. At least, he reasoned to himself, I got the words right. Just not in the right order.

With his part of the play done, he joined the snowflakes and trees, chattering his teeth the loudest. He howled wind like a baying hound and snapped his fingers furiously in a snow flurry. He trembled from the cold.

The play ended with Alfonso saying that if they came back to life, the Donner party would be sorry for eating each other. "It's just not right," he argued. "You gotta suck it up in bad times."

Robert figured that Alfonso was right. He remembered how one day his sister had locked him in the closet, and he didn't eat or drink for five hours. When he got out he hit his sister, but not so hard as to leave a bruise. He then ate three sandwiches and felt a whole lot better.

The cast then paraded up the aisle into the audience. Belinda pinched Robert hard, but only once because she was thinking that it could have been worse. As he passed a smiling and relieved Mrs. Bunnin, she patted Robert's shoulder and said, "Almost perfect."

Robert was happy. He'd made it through without passing out from fear. Now the first and second graders were looking at him and clapping. He was sure everyone wondered who the actor was behind that smooth voice and red, red beard.

# About Gary Soto

••••••••

I am of Mexican descent and was raised in Fresno, California. I was no good at school. I could not sing, do art, or figure out math problems. I was deathly scared of the stage, yet jealous when my friends got up on the stage and sang with gusto. I graduated from high school with a meager 1.6 grade-point average, but managed to go to college, first at Fresno City College and later California State University at Fresno, where I fooled everyone by graduating magna cum laude. During these years I roomed with my brother, Rick, an artist, and an assortment of poor college students. It was the waning days of cheap living, when it was possible to rent an entire flat for eighty-five dollars.

Some of my favorite verbals are eating, sleeping, and reading. I also like to walk, but not far, and I like to lift weights, but not heavy ones. I like to play sports, especially basketball and karate. I have traveled widely, but like to sleep in my own bed. Unlike my daughter, Mariko, an eighth grader, I am scared of horses.

I am a poet, essayist, and a young-adult writer. My first book was *The Elements of San Joaquin*, a poetry collection that explores the relationship between place and family. My other poetry collections include *Black Hair, A Fire in My Hands*, and *Who Will Know Us?* I have written about the Mexican-American experience in my books *Living Up the Street* and *A Summer Life*. I have made a short film, *The Bike*. I have won numerous awards for my writing, including fellowships from the Guggenheim Foundation, the National Endowment for the Arts, and the California Arts Council. I teach at the University of California, Berkeley.